All He Ever Needed

Tay Mo'Nae

Stay up to date with Tay Mo'Nae

Want to stay up to date with my work? Be the first to get sneak peeks, release dates, cover reveals, character updates, and more?
Join my Facebook reading group: Tay's Book Baes, and like my like page: Tay Mo'Nae.
Make sure you check my website out for updates as well:
Taymonaewrites.com
Also, join my **mailing list** for exclusive firsts by texting **AuthorTay** to **33777**

Prologue

Prologue

I ndigo wiped the back of her forehead with her hand and looked around the final room of the house she had just finished cleaning. Since she had schoolwork to complete earlier in the day, she started her work day later than normal. It was nearing ten at night, and she was finally finished for the day.

Indigo had been working as a maid for Silas for a little over a year now, and so far she had no complaints. His three-bedroom condo was the typical bachelor pad that she spent four times a week cleaning. When she wasn't here she was at school.

Indigo was at the end of her master's program where she would be completing her chemistry degree. She didn't want to rely on anyone to pay for her schooling. She had qualified for a few scholarships, and the remaining part of her school balance she handled herself, which was why she took up a job. The last thing she wanted was to be in debt before she even started her career. Being a maid wasn't ideal, but the hours worked with her schooling, and they weren't demanding. She was able to study and stay on top of her schoolwork, and her boss wasn't too bad.

Reaching up, Indigo pulled her shoulder-length, blonde and choco-late locs out the low ponytail they were in and eyed the living room. It was the last room on her list today. Silas had threw some kind of gathering the day before and left it unkempt. She knew it would take the most time so she had focused on the other rooms first, then tackled this one.

When Indigo first took on the job, she expected her boss to live in some huge mansion and was shocked when his assistant sent her to this location. Not that the condo wasn't luxurious and spacious, but for who Silas was, she thought he would have something larger.

The condo had three bedrooms and three and a half baths. There was a study, gym, kitchen, dining room, and a terrace with a pool.

Since she was finished for the day, she planned on collecting her things and heading to her townhouse so she could get a little studying in before calling it a night.

Her attention was caught by the opening of the front door and beeping of the alarm. Indigo knew it couldn't have been anyone but Silas. He had a private garage that housed his cars and the elevator only traveled to his condo.

A thump caused her to spin around. She tried to stay out Silas' sight as much as possible. Not because she didn't like him or anything. In fact, it was the complete opposite. She knew it wasn't professional to lust after her boss, but she couldn't help it.

With walnut skin, a bulky muscular built, broad shoulders, tone arms, and wide chest, Silas was hard to ignore when he was in the room.

Right now he was laughing at whoever was on the other side of his phone. His naturally hazel, hooded eyes closed, causing small crinkles on the side of them.

Indigo scanned her boss over. Dressed in a dark gray tailored suit, she watched as he loosened his tie and kicked off his shoes.

"Yeah, man. I'll get right on that." Silas' deep baritone rang through her ears. "Fuck you, I got this."

He hung up on whoever was on the phone and slid his phone into his pocket. When he lifted his head, Indigo's body stilled when his greenish, brown orbs fell on her.

"Shit." He stumbled back slightly before squinting his eyes. "I didn't know you were still here." Silas stepped away from his door and started towards where Indigo was near his charcoal gray couch.

"I had a late day today because I had school. Fiona said it was okay," Indigo let him know, referring to his assistant. She hardly dealt with him; usually, all her communication went through Fiona.

Tucking his plump bottom lip between his straight white teeth, Silas nodded his head. Creases formed on her forehead.

"Right." He shrugged and looked around his open living room. "Looks good."

When his eyes landed back on her, a crooked grin formed on his face.

"I'll be out your hair soon. I just gotta grab my things and then—"

"Stay," he blurted out, shocking her. "I feel like you be running from me. Any time I'm home and you're here, you're quick to leave." He snatched the tie he was wearing looser.

"I don't know what you're talking about." She watched him carefully. Her heart pounded loudly in her ears. Truthfully, she always felt like she was a dog in heat around Silas. He screamed BDE, and his cockiness was oddly an even more turn-on for her.

Indigo took the moment to take him in again. He kept his hair cut low, chin hair low, and mustache above his heart-shaped, pink lips lined up.

She cleared her throat. "Uh, I don't think that's appropriate." His wide nose scrunched for a second before he grinned.

"Nonsense. You're finished, right?"

Indigo bobbed her head.

"Then chill. Have a drink with me. I should learn a little about the woman who spends more time at my house than me."

Something told Indigo she should've turned down his offer. Going home and studying was safer, but there was a small nagging in her stomach that told her to live a little. Indigo always stayed on the straight and narrow. School was always her main focus. She dated some and went out with girlfriends here and there, but school was always the first priority. She wasn't as spontaneous as most people her age.

"Okay," she agreed after an internal debate.

Silas' mouth heighted. "Good. What would you like?" He turned and headed for the bar in his dining room.

"Whatever you're having."

For a second, Silas paused. He glanced over his shoulder with one of his bushy brows raised. "Rolling with the big dogs. I got you," he spoke with a sly grin that made butterflies flutter in her stomach.

———

Two Old Fashions later, both Silas and Indigo were buzzed, and the awkwardness in the room had fled.

He had already had a couple drinks before coming home and now these drinks were catching up to him. Silas had a high tolerance for alcohol, and he had tried to cut back on drinking so much, but he'd had a long day today. One of the deals he had been working on wasn't going how he liked, and his parents were on his back more than usual. Both caused him to drink more than normal. He had took a couple shots at work by his lonesome before calling for his car to take him home.

Silas was the CEO of Culture Ties Media, the largest multimedia company on the East Coast.

With low drunken eyes, Silas turned and eyed the maid who had been working for him the past year. Since Fiona first introduced Indigo to him, he was attracted to her.

It was a struggle coming home and smelling her sweet perfume lingering in his house and not being able to touch her.

Indigo was average height, caramel skin, and small but curvy at the same time. Her hips were wide, waist small, and her ass was like a full moon.

Silas' dick twitched as he scanned her face over. Her dark, slanted eyes were more slanted than normal, and her full cupid bow lips were pulled into a pouty grin. She kept giggling and apologizing which Silas thought was cute.

For the past year, he had pictured what it would be like to bed his maid and tonight, he wasn't sure how much self-control he could continue to have. With the stress from work building up and no sexual release in over a month, he was stressed out.

"You got a man, Indigo?" Silas asked.

A person in his position couldn't be fighting a nigga over a woman he only wanted one night with. He didn't know much about the maid, but he knew he wanted her.

Her mouth snapped shut and eyes widened while her cheeks flushed more than they already were.

"What? No." She shook her head.

A crooked grin formed on his face. "Good. That means ain't no issue if I do this." Before Indigo could question him, he was moving and placing his lips on hers.

He could tell he caught her off guard at first. Her body stiffened where she sat, but it didn't take long for her to fall in line.

The kiss grew heated and their tongues tangled with one another. The taste of alcohol she had been consuming seemed to intoxicate him more. His tongue caressed the inside of her mouth.

A small moan fled her mouth, entering his.

She grabbed his shirt since he had stripped out his suit and gripped it tightly.

Silas knew he wanted more, but he had to do this correctly. The last thing he needed was a sexual harassment case.

"Are you drunk?" he asked, pulling away. Indigo's lips were now more swollen. and her breathing was heavier.

She shook her head. "Buzzed not drunk."

"And you want this? You're able to consent?"

He watched her chest rise and fall quickly. Her small, pink tongue darted out and swiped her lips.

"Consent to what?" Her words slightly slurred, and her eyes smoldered with heat.

"I want to fuck you," he told her boldly. Silas was never the one to mince words. With the way he was raised, he always said what was on his mind and went for what he wanted.

A small chuckle fell from his mouth when her eyes looked like they would pop out the socket.

Licking his lips, he scooted closer to her, and his knees brushed against hers. "Is that okay with you?" His finger brushed down her arm, causing goosebumps to form.

She batted her lashes and struggled to form her next words.

Silas's dick twitched in his slacks. His eyes focused on hers lips. Seeing she wasn't gonna reply right away, he moved in and pressed his lips against hers. His fingers still brushed up and down her arms.

Her body sagged closer to his, and her eyes closed. Silas tugged on her bottom lip, sucking it into his mouth.

"Can I take you to my bed and have my way with you?" His voice was thick and throaty.

Pulling back again, he studied her.

Indigo, still lost for words, moved her head up and down.

Using his pointer finger, he grabbed and placed it under her chin. "I need words."

Indigo swallowed hard; her eyes fluttered. She grabbed her glass and threw the remaining liquid back. Her eyes were clear and focused.

"Yes. Take me."

Grinning, that was all Silas needed. The liquor was taking more of an affect. His body blazed and his dick begged to be between something warm and snug.

———

After gaining her consent, Silas moved on auto pilot. Quickly, they moved to his bedroom and Silas wasted no time undressing her and kissing on her luscious skin. Her hands roamed over his broad shoulders and her back arched.

His tongue swirled around her hardened nipples while his hands explored her body.

She gasped when he covered her breast with his hot mouth and sucked on it. When his hand went between her legs, he couldn't help but groan after feeling how wet she was. His thick fingers brushed over her lower lips a couple times before invading her walls. They were snug, and she slightly winced when he pushed it further inside her.

Pulling up and releasing her breast with a loud pop, Silas stared at Indigo with a drunken smirk on his face.

She rolled her hips into his fingers with her bottom lip sucked between her teeth. When she arched her back again, the smooth part of her neck called for him and begged him to taste.

Dipping his head low, he covered her skin and pulled it into his mouth. Another one of his fingers invaded her walls.

"Oohhh!" she whined, wiggling her hips.

His dick was harder than a brick and pressed against her thighs. One of her hands cuffed the back of his head as he hungrily attacked her neck.

Indigo's body trembled beneath him and her juices flooded his fingers. She cried out as she came and the sounds were now embedded into his mind.

When he couldn't take anymore, he hurried and lifted up. Indigo was breathing heavily and panting softly. Her eyes were shut as Silas stripped out the rest of his suit. He grabbed a condom from his bedside table and covered his thick shaft.

Climbing back on his California king bed, he hovered over Indigo and bent down. His tongue traced over her lips and he lined himself at her entrance.

Pressing her lips into his, Indigo wrapped her arms around his shoulders. Her body jerked and she cried out when he pushed himself into her, not gentle at all. Her nails sunk into his shoulders.

His strokes were strong and deep. He gritted and dipped his head by how tight she was hugging his shaft.

Silas knew he was a nice size, but the way he was stretching her and she was hugging his dick had him about to cum too quickly.

He paused, shifting his hips and pulled up. He noticed her eyes squeezed shut and mouth pinched tightly when he grabbed her thighs and pushed her legs up.

A loud moan fell from her lips when he was able to go deeper inside her.

Silas tested her flexibility and stroked her slowly at first. Her breast bounced as her body jerked from his thrust.

Indigo's body was tensed at first but she loosened as Silas fucked her. He worked her body over until both of them were drained.

Indigo had cum multiple times, and her throat felt raw by the time they were finished.

When they were finished, Silas' body felt lighter, his balls were empty, and the tension he felt was barely existent.

A relationship or anything permanent wasn't anything he was looking for but since Indigo worked for him, he couldn't just disregard her like he normally did. Thankfully, he didn't have to figure out how to get her out his bed because Indigo started collecting her things, preparing for her leave on her own.

"You need my driver to take you home?" he asked her after silence became awkward. He might not have wanted anything past the sex they'd just had, but he didn't want her to crash while driving home.

Without looking at him, she shook her head. "At least sleep in one of the guest rooms until you sober up."

She paused with her clothes in hand. "We drunk a lot tonight, and I don't want you to hurt yourself or anyone else," he said.

Indigo didn't look at him but nodded and started for the door. He watched her, wondering if he had fucked up. Indigo was a great employee. She kept his house spotless and never gave him any issues. He would've hated to lose her because she couldn't keep her feelings in check.

Sighing, his hand dragged down his face; that was something he would worry about another time. The liquor had took over and his eyes were heavy. Tonight's problems could be handled tomorrow.

Chapter One

Indigo

Currently, I was sitting in Java Books with my books scattered across the table, notebook opened, and highlighter in hand. I had a paper for the lab we did in one of my classes due in two days and hadn't started yet.

The past week, I hadn't been on my game which was so unlike me. Part of me knew my body was telling me I needed to slow down. Exhaustion had been hovering over me the past few days, but I couldn't slow down.

I was still working at Silas' four days a week, which after our night together, I thought would be weird but thankfully, it wasn't. He didn't come home until late at night, and I was typically gone by four—five the latest. My second half of spring semester had started and this time, outside of the lab I had every Tuesday, all my classes were online. We always had a paper due by Friday in the same class. Normally, I was on top of it, but like I mentioned it had been a slow week.

Rubbing my eyes and slightly squinting them, I tried to focus on my notes in front of me. I reached for the frozen latte in front of me, hoping the caffeine would wake me up.

After another hour of suffering, I had finally managed to highlight and make note of everything I would need to include within my paper when my phone buzzed next to me, pausing the music playing in my headphones.

Inwardly, I groaned after seeing my sister's name on the screen. I loved her but I knew if she was calling, it was because she wanted to gossip or wanted a favor.

"Answer," I spoke to my AirPods.

Setting my highlighter down, I picked up my phone and stared at the screen.

"Hey, sis!" Charley grinned into the phone.

"Hey." I yawned while covering my mouth.

"What are you doing?"

"Studying."

Charley bunched her face up. "Boo, that's so boring. Come out with me."

"It's Thursday for one, Charley, and for two, I have to finish this paper."

She rolled her eyes, causing me to snicker. "Today's half-off night at Blue Smoke, let's go get some drinks, have some wings, and catch up. It'll only be for a few hours. God, I miss my sister."

A smile formed on my face. My sister, who was younger than me by three years, was so dramatic. "Charley, just wait 'til the weekend. I really have to finish this paper and—"

"No, please, sis! You know you love their wings, and I'll buy the first round of drinks." She poked her bottom lip out.

Glancing down at the table, I ran my eyes over everything I'd accomplished today. I had been here for hours doing homework and studying. All that was left to do was type up the paper, and since I had everything lined up already, it wouldn't take me too long.

"Fine." I groaned and rolled my eyes.

"Oh stop! If I know you, you need a break anyways."

"Whatever. I'm going to run home and drop my things off then I'll meet you there."

"Okay! See you soon."

When we hung up, I placed my hand on my stomach. The coffee was starting to get to me, proving I'd probably overdone it. I hadn't eaten all day outside of one of the premade sandwiches the coffee shop offered.

"Wings sound good," I muttered as I gathered my things.

———

"See, aren't you happy that I dragged you out?" Charley questioned, sipping on the colored drink in her glass.

Playfully rolling my eyes, I brought the hookah tip to my mouth and inhaled the fruit punch flavor. "Whatever, Charley, you're lucky I needed a break." Lifting my mouth up, I blew the smoke out.

"Well, I'm for one glad you agreed. I feel like all you do is study!" my cousin, but more like my sister, Audrey spoke.

"You know, Big Sis has always been all work and no play! Books, books, books. That's all she ever cared about."

"That's not true! My major is just demanding, so I have to buckle down more. I'm drawing to the end of my degree though, so I'll have a little more free time once I'm done."

"It's been a long time coming too. I miss my partner in crime," Audrey whined before downing her lemon drop.

"I know that's right." The three of us laughed.

Not only was Audrey an only child, but her parents worked a lot too growing up so she spent a lot of time at my house hanging out with me and Charley. Although Charley was only twenty-three, she still was my best friend growing up. We never went through the whole annoying little sister thing. My parents raised us to be close, and Audrey fit right in. Growing up, we were often called The Three Musketeers.

Just as I was about to speak, a weird taste filled the back of my throat causing me to throw my hand to my mouth. I closed my eyes and rubbed between my breasts.

"You okay?" Charley asked.

Not responding right away, I rubbed the irritation in my chest away and swallowed down the vile taste.

"Indi?"

I shook my head. "I'm good; just had a flash of heartburn." I cleared my throat and grabbed my drink, taking a sip. "Where are those wings?" I frowned and looked around.

Blue Smoke had the best wings in the city. A lot of people came here just for them alone.

"So there's a speed dating event that dating app *Love Connections* is hosting next weekend. We should all go!" Audrey threw out there.

My nose scrunched up. "Why would we do that?"

"Because we're all single, and I don't know about y'all, but I'm ready to have steady dick in my life."

"I heard that!" Charley slapped hands with her.

The mention of dick made me think of Silas and the night we spent together. It'd been over a month and I still had flashbacks of it. He was thick between his legs, average length, but his dick filled every area of my pussy. Each time he dug into me, I felt like he was trying to find gold, going deeper and deeper.

My thighs clenched together.

"I don't have time to go speed dating. I have exams coming up soon and two end-of-the-term papers to finish. I graduate next month so these next couple weeks, I must buckle down."

Both my sister and cousin looked at each other, rolling their eyes. "Boring!"

Smirking, I finished up my drink just as the server of our table brought our food.

"Can I get a Sprite, please?" I asked her, rubbing my chest again. I don't know where this sudden heartburn came from but it needed to go away.

"Well, we'll leave Miss Bookworm alone. I'm down. I'm off next weekend anyways."

"Well, you two have fun for me."

The night continued with my sister and cousin, and I couldn't deny I was having a good time out. I had been throwing myself into my schoolwork hard lately, and I didn't remember the last time I went out and enjoyed myself.

Once the night was over, I drove a couple blocks over to where my townhouse was in Sunset Developments.

"Shit." I groaned the moment I was in the bathroom. I didn't think I drank too much, but what I did have was going right through me.

I glanced at the clock on the wall. It was nearing eleven at night. I still had to shower and then type my paper. It was due by twelve p.m. tomorrow afternoon.

Yawning, I wiped and washed my hands then stripped out the rest of my clothes. My sister and cousin's concerns filled my thoughts as I stepped in the shower and the hot water hit me. I was always so tired and maybe I did need to slow down some, but I was so close to the finish line, I knew there was no way I could without falling behind.

"One more month," I mumbled, grabbing my Goddess Glow body wash and applying it to my loofah.

It had been a long time coming and a lot of long draining nights, but it would be worth it once my degree was in hand.

Chapter Two

Silas

"Ayra sent back the contract earlier this afternoon and Be Bold Network has also renewed the contract there with us," Fiona let me know.

I glanced away from my computer at her with my brows bunched. "Who's Ayra?'

An annoyed expression formed on her face, causing me to smirk. Fiona had been working for me for the past five years, and she was the best assistant I could ask for. Without her I was sure I would go crazy.

"Ayra owns Issa Vibe Magazine. She's looking to expand the brand of the magazine and expand her online presence."

"Right." I nodded, still lost.

I tried to be somewhat in tune with all the things Culture Ties Media had going on and the people we worked with. As the largest Black multimedia company on the East Coast, I prided myself with making sure all the companies we worked with succeeded.

Before we could go further, my phone vibrated on my desk. Glancing down at it, I inwardly groaned after seeing my mom's name displayed. This was the third time she called, and I knew if I kept dodging her, she would've made an in-person appearance.

Fiona snickered when she glanced at my phone. "Good luck with that."

My scowl deepened.

I watched as she turned and headed out my office. I could already feel the headache forming before I answered.

"Hey, Mom." I finally picked up.

Placing the phone between my shoulder and ear, I turned back to my computer.

"Silas, you know that's not how you answer the phone." I pictured the disapproving look on her face.

Sighing, I closed my eyes and counted to ten. "What can I do for you, Mother?"

"Why do I feel like I need to go on a hunt whenever I want to speak to my only son? It's been a while since you've been by the house to see me and your father. Not to mention you never answer the phone. You're not avoiding your parents, are you?"

Sitting straight, I brought my finger to my temple and massaged it.

I loved my parents, I truly did, but it wasn't always easy being their kid. Both my parents came from old money. A lot of the time my dad was in his own world, barely present in what I had going on, but my mother, on the other hand, was the opposite. She wanted to be too invested in my life.

The moment my trust fund hit from my paternal grandparents at twenty-one, I took the money and started Culture Ties Media.

"Of course not, Mother. I do run a very successful business, and I don't always have time to come visit."

She made a displeasing sound. "We are your parents, Silas, and we live in the same city. It won't kill you to make some time to come visit."

Just as I was about to speak, she continued.

"We're having dinner with the Wentworths this Friday, and I expect you to come."

"Mom."

"It's non-negotiable, Silas. Make sure you wear your best and be on time, seven sharp. Now, I have a facial I'm to walk into. I'll see you Friday."

Before I could turn down the invitation, I heard the click of the call ending. Sagging my shoulders forward, I shook my head and allowed my phone to fall onto my lap. I should have known I could only avoid Pamela Newton for so long.

Knowing there was nothing I could do now, I decided to push it to the back of my mind. It was Wednesday and tonight, I met with the guys for our weekly darts night. I was ready to unwind for the day.

——

"The world must be ending. We been here for almost an hour and you've barely said a word," Caspian commented.

I walked back to the high table after throwing my darts and took a seat, grabbing my Old Fashion and tossing it back.

"Just been a long day, nothing major." I waved him off.

I glanced over and saw Lawson in his phone. "You talking about me, but this nigga ain't put his phone down since we got here."

Caspian chuckled. "We all know he over there pillow talking. Yo' wife not going anywhere, Law. Enjoy your time out." Caspian slapped his shoulder.

Lawson glanced up when we all laughed. "To hell with y'all. Just 'cause y'all gon' be lonely old men, don't be mad at me."

"Shit, who's lonely?"

"Who's old? Well, besides Rhys ass," I joked.

Rhys turned from the dart board and flicked me off. "I personally think what you and Zarinah have is beautiful. I been considering settling down myself," he continued once he was back at the table.

My face scrunched. "Why would you want to do that? Being tied down to a nagging woman doesn't sound pleasant."

"My wife doesn't nag." Lawson cut his eyes at me.

I waved him off. "All women nag. Not to mention, once you settle down, women want to start having kids then you have no free time. I'm good on all that. I like being able to come and go as I please."

"You're wrong, man," Lawson stated, setting his phone on the table. "My wife and daughter bring so much joy to my life. I love seeing my daughter grow every day, and it's nice having someone to come home to every night. You're missing out."

"Shit, I'm about to be thirty-five with three Super Bowls under my belt. It's about time I settle down. I'm not getting younger." Rhys' shoulders lifted.

"With how much my mom be on my case, I'll probably never settle down." My brows furrowed and forehead creased. I was sure that's what this dinner was about Friday. I was sure my mom was gonna try and force one of her friends' daughters on me like she has multiple times.

"Don't worry, Si, I'm not looking to settle down anytime soon," Caspian spoke up.

I glanced at my friend. "Good. I need someone who still has their balls."

"I got my balls and they stay emptied every night." Lawson stood and headed for the dartboard.

"TMI, dude."

I waved the guy in the bowtie over for another drink.

It always felt good to get together with the guys. Every week we met at The Raven. Being that we been friends since childhood, and high school for Rhys, we'd been through a lot of shit together. We started this dart team years ago, and even though the older we got the busier we all seemed to get, we always made sure to get together to forget our stressful lives.

———

One would think I would be comfortable in the house I grew up in but it was always the complete opposite. Growing up, my house never felt like a home. There was no warm, welcoming, familiar feeling either.

Currently, I was sitting at the dining room table with my parents and the Wentworths. I was unable to get out of the dinner, so instead I was counting down until I could make my escape.

Just like I expected, Dad was tuned out, not paying attention to anything surrounding him while Mom hadn't stopped speaking since everyone sat down.

"You know Steve and Beth's daughter, Spencer, is single Silas," my mom commented, gaining my attention.

First frowning at my mom, I looked towards the Wentworths. Beth was around my mom's age, in her mid-fifties, but she had a lot of work done to her face. You could tell she loved Botox a little too much and her lips were overly filled. Steve was balding and had plugs that didn't blend too well.

I blinked a few times. "That's nice to hear."

"Yes, Spencer is away right now in Italy, but when she returns, I'm sure she'll be happy see you again," Beth commented.

"It has been some years since the two of you seen each other. You know I always thought you looked good together." My mom grinned.

My mouth pinched together. She was never subtle with anything.

"Steve is looking to step down in his position this year, and Spencer is next to take over since she is the oldest of the Wentworth children. Beth was telling me they were hoping she would marry before that happened."

Giving my mom a blank stare, I tilted my head to the side. "I hope she finds someone."

"Silas!" my mom chastised with a laughed. Her eyes narrowed. "Spencer has mentioned wanting to catch up with you, and I told Beth you would feel the same."

"And why would you do that, Mother?"

I could tell it was taking everything in my mom not to lose her cool. She always wanted to be 'put together' and in control with company present.

"So, Steve... I was thinking about hitting the green tomorrow morning," my dad finally made himself known.

"Unfortunately, my Spencer isn't getting any younger. If she wants to have kids, time is of the essence. She hasn't had the best of luck with men, so I promised to step in and help her."

"And since you can't find a respectable woman to settle down with, we agreed the two of you would be perfect for each other."

I closed my eyes and pushed a heavy breath out. I don't know why I was shocked by this ambush by my mother. I knew she was pushing for me to settle down and have kids, but this was getting out of control.

"I don't need any help finding a woman, Mother. I haven't settled down because I don't want to." When I opened my eyes, I bounced them between my mom and Beth's.

She looked put off by my words. "Nonsense, Silas. A man of your stature looks bad being unwed and heirless. It's time for you to take your future more serious."

"I tell my Spencer the same thing."

Instead of continuing to go back and forth with them, I pulled my phone out. I ate before I arrived, knowing I would lose my appetite at some point of the evening.

"No phones at the table, Silas," my mom scolded.

"Actually, I gotta go." I stood up, locking my phone. "Something has come up."

"Silas," my mom commented.

Ignoring her, I went and kissed her cheek then nodded my head at the rest of the table. "It was nice seeing you all." My dad was still in deep conversation with Steve, and my mom looked like she was two seconds away from blowing a gasket.

I would hear her mouth the next time I heard from her, but I would deal with that later. My mom needed to learn to stay in her lane.

Quickly, I left out the dining room and down the long hallway leading to the front of the house. I didn't even have anything going on, but I wasn't sitting at the table another minute.

Chapter Three

Indigo

"S uck in," my sister demanded as she tried to zip the white halter top dress that was supposed to be under my gown.

Today was the day I worked so hard for. My graduation day. The past couple weeks were brutal, and I felt as if I was gonna crash and burn more than once, but I pushed through it. Now it was time to celebrate all the hard work I put in.

"I am!" I whined. "Maybe I got the wrong size."

Charley huffed. "Indi, the dress isn't zipping up. I think you'll have to wear something else."

"I don't have anything else!"

I looked at myself in the mirror and watched as my sister struggled to zip the dress up. "Doesn't it have a clasp at the top? Try and do that first then zip."

Inhaling a deep breath, I watched her and waited. "Okay there. Shit, Indi. Maybe think about going up a size next time." She stepped away from me with her mouth upside down.

Rolling my eyes, I stepped forward and took a look at myself. "Even your boobs are bigger." Charley poked one with her finger.

"Stop!" I slapped her hand away.

She snickered. "I'm just saying. You're looking thick, sis." Rolling my eyes, again, I ran my eyes over myself. I had to blink a couple times seeing how high my boobs sat up in this dress. The dress did seem to give them a little extra push-up.

I grabbed the mid-section of the dress and adjusted it. It felt kind of tight, but I ignored it. Yesterday, I had went and got my hair retwisted and washed. I chose not to wear any makeup outside of some nude lipstick with lip gloss over it.

"Okay, I'm about to go in the living room and wait with everyone else while you finish."

I nodded. "Okay."

It didn't take long for me to finish up. I made sure to grab my cap and gown out my closet and the tan wedges I was gonna wear for the day. Right now, I had some flip flops on and was gonna change them at the college.

"Look at my baby," my mom gushed once I stepped inside my living room.

Next to her was my dad beaming at me with pride. The both of them stood up. They were wearing shirts with my face on the front and 'Congrats Grad' on the back. "Please don't start, Mom," I groaned.

"Let me have my moment. You worked so hard for this, and I'm so proud of you!" I stepped closer to them.

"We both are." My parents enveloped me in their embrace.

"You refused any handouts and did this all on your own. Me and your mother were afraid you might kill yourself studying too hard, but you did it." My dad kissed my temple.

I stepped back.

"A'right, pictures." My mom clapped and grabbed her phone.

Groaning again, I shook my head. "Mom."

"Just give your mother this, Indigo."

"Yeah c'mon on, sis!" Charley grabbed me.

My townhouse was equipped with a fireplace and Charley pulled me over to it.

My mom came over with us. "Put your cap and gown on!" she complained.

Sighing, I did as she said. My mom waited for me to do what she said before snapping a few pictures.

"Don't leave me out!" Audrey complained, hurrying over.

We got a couple shots together and then I got some solo ones. My mom and dad made sure to get some with me.

"Okay, okay. I feel like this is high school all over again," I told them and glanced at the time. "I need to be heading to the school anyways."

"I wish your brother was here for this. I would have loved to get one with all you together," my mom muttered while looking through the photos we took.

My younger brother, Myles, was away at his first year of college. He had some end of the year assignment to finish up and couldn't get away for today.

Butterflies filled my stomach. I was excited for graduation, but I was nervous at the same time. This had been a long time coming, and now, everything was paying off.

———

My foot tapped rapidly and my stomach flipped as I waited for my name to be called. I rubbed the center of my chest. For some reason, over the past few weeks, I'd been having heartburn like crazy.

My hands went to my thighs, and I rubbed them over my black gown.

The names were being called and it was getting closer to my turn. Families and friends cheers piled through the stadium, overshadowing the announcer's voice. It was a joyous day for everyone.

When I heard my section called, my heart doubled in speed as we all stood up.

"Whoa, you okay?" the guy behind me asked when I stumbled.

Blinking a couple times, I shook the hazy feeling away. "Yeah." I smiled lightly. "Just stood too quick. It made me a little light-headed."

I brushed the back of my hand over my forehead.

Facing forward, I felt my pulse picking up the closer it got to my turn. So many times I was ready to give up and say forget it. Getting your master's in chemistry with a minor in chemical engineering wasn't easy. It took a lot of studying, but I always had a passion for science. Growing up, it was the one subject I always looked.forward to. At twenty-seven, I was finally about to start my dream career.

I glanced up and swiped my tongue over my lips. There was only one person before me.

I inhaled a deep breath and slowly pushed it out.

Don't trip.

Don't trip.

I wasn't normally a klutz, but I always worried about falling in situations like this.

Get it together, Indigo.

The moment my name was called, I pushed all the negative thoughts out my head. I grinned and walked up the steps. I could hear my family cheering loudly for me along with my classmates and other attendees clapping for me.

The lights were beaming down on us, and I had to blink a few times as my eyes adjusted to them.

Smiling, I approached the dean and grabbed her outreached hand, giving it a shake and posing for a picture as she handed me the holder for my degree.

"Congratulations." She smiled at me.

With a small nod, I bypassed her and shook the head of my department's hand and posed for a picture as well.

I stepped away from him and felt like a weight had been lifted off my shoulders. So many long, sleepless nights and they were finally paying off. My social life had took a small dive the past few months since I was so focused on ending my semester on a high note. It all paid off since I ended up making the dean's list, but I could tell my body was begging for some rest. I'd neglected taking care of myself like I should.

Out of nowhere, a flash of heat passed through me. I was close to walking off the stage when my vision became blurry and suddenly, things went black.

———

Groaning, my eyes fluttered open and my body felt heavy.

"Indigo, honey." I heard my mom's voice.

Squinting, I slowly opened my eyes, and it took a couple seconds for them to get adjusted to the lights above me.

"Mom?" I questioned.

I heard light beeps around me.

When my eyes fully adjusted, I saw my parents, sister, and Audrey all surrounding me. The looks on their faces were ones I couldn't quite make out.

"Graduation!" I suddenly blurted out, remembering what today was.

I went to sit up but my mom stopped me. "Relax. Graduation is over and you're at the hospital."

My nose scrunched up. "Hospital?" I looked around. Then, I remembered being on stage and then nothing.

"You passed out. Gave us all a scare," my dad commented.

"That's embarrassing," I groaned, closing my eyes.

Here I was nervous about falling and I took it to the extreme. However, it did explain why my head was pounding.

When I opened my eyes, I narrowed them. "What's wrong?" I looked between everyone. They all still had a look on their face as if there was more.

"Y'all don't have to worry, I'm not dying. I've been going hard these past few weeks because of papers and exams. I haven't been taking care of myself. I'm probably just dehydrated." I lifted the arm with the IV in it. "See, fluids."

Still, no one spoke.

A sinking filling filled my stomach as I studied each person's expression.

"Indi," my mom started. She grabbed my hand. "How come you didn't tell us you were expecting?"

I snatched my hand from her as if it was on fire. "Expecting? Expecting what?" My brows furrowed together and nose scrunched.

"A baby! How could you not tell us!" my sister complained.

I opened my mouth to tell them they were crazy just as the curtain was being pulled back. Turning my attention forward, I noticed a middle-aged Black man stepping inside.

"I'm glad to see you're up. I'm Dr. Arnolds. How are you feeling?" he asked, walking to the hand sanitizer on the wall and applying some to his hands.

"I would be better if I didn't wake up to my family talking crazy. They seem to think I'm pregnant."

The doctor turned to face me with a confused look. "Are you telling me you weren't aware you were carrying?"

He might as well have told me dinosaurs were walking the earth by how I was looking at him. "Carrying? You've got it confused. I'm not...I can't be." My voice trailed off while seeing the serious expression on his face.

Suddenly, it was like I'd swallowed sand. I looked around the small room at my family who were studying me.

"Indi." My mom grabbed my hand, but I snatched away again.

"No. I can't be pregnant. I just graduated. I start my job in two weeks!"

One of my professors, that I looked to as a mentor, had set me up with an entry level job in my field, which was a blessing. I was worried how long it could take me to get hired after I finished school, but she presented me with this opportunity a month before graduation.

"Just take a couple breaths," my dad coached.

I shook my head. "There's got to be a mistake."

Dr. Arnolds went to the computer in the room and logged in. He cleared his throat. "Outside of being dehydrated and your iron being low, everything seemed to be okay. I ordered an ultrasound for when you woke up so we can check on the baby and determine how far along you are."

I had drowned the doctor out by this point. I was still stuck on the fact that he was claiming I was pregnant. He had to be wrong and confused my test with someone else. It'd been months since I had sex and if I was pregnant, I would have known, right? I tried to think if I had any clues that I was carrying. My life had been on go for months now, and I barely had time to blink.

The next hour went by in a blur. I remember speaking and hearing people talk to me, but I could barely comprehend what was going on.

"Three months! How are you three months and didn't know!" Audrey asked.

"Well that explains the weight gain," Charley followed up.

I cut my eyes at both of them. "I can't deal with this right now." I rubbed my eyes and shook my head.

"Well, I'm for one excited! I can't wait to meet my grandbaby!" my mom gushed.

My dad wrapped his arm around my shoulder and kissed my temple. "Everyone relax. Can't y'all give the girl sometime to adjust to the news?"

I glanced up at him with a thankful expression on my face. Everything was moving too fast. Here I was preparing to start my life and a wrench suddenly got thrown in my plans.

My family ended up giving me my privacy so I could get dressed. I was in the middle of pulling my dress up when I froze.

On top of everything else the realization hit me. Not only was I was pregnant, but I was pregnant with my boss's baby.

Chapter Four

Silas

After pulling my jeans up, I reached for my shirt and slid it over my head. I heard movement behind me, indicating Ria doing the same thing.

"I hope it doesn't take you a million years to call next time," she spoke as I prepared to leave.

Smirking, I glanced at her over my shoulder. "We'll see. You're the one that's tied down." I nodded towards her left hand. She rolled her eyes and pulled her dress up.

"Yeah, well it's not like he's ever home."

Shaking my head, I reached over for my keys and phone so I could leave.

When Ria and I first started hooking up, I wasn't aware she was married. By the time it had come out, we had already slept together a couple times. She didn't care about her marriage, so I didn't see the point to stop. Her husband was always out of town, and she assured me he wouldn't care even if he did know. Apparently, they had an open marriage since he was always traveling. It wasn't my business anyways; we only met up a couple times every so many months. I never asked questions about her marriage and she never offered information.

In my position, it was draining trying to hook up with random women whenever I wanted. Too many times I'd had women get the wrong idea or try and trap me into something I didn't want. My life was too busy to settle down, and I wasn't looking for anything serious at the moment either. My goal at the moment was to continue to build my company and make money. Never did I want to rely on my parents' wealth.

Discreetly, I left out the hotel room and made my way to the steps. I would take the elevator from the floor below.

Taking the elevator to the parking garage where my car was, I pulled my phone out and scanned through my notifications.

We had met up at *MK Hotel and Casino* in Butter Ridge Falls. I didn't want to meet in New Haven in case someone recognized me.

Once in my Aston Martin, I pushed the button and instantly rolled down the window and pulled out. Lil Wayne blared through my speakers as I bobbed my head and headed back to New Haven. I had to stop by the office before heading home for the day.

Halfway to the city, my music was paused and on the screen I saw that my mom was calling, so I didn't hesitate to ignore it. I hadn't spoke to her since walking out on dinner a couple weeks back. All she was calling for was to scold me about embarrassing her in front of the Wentworths. You would think after the multiple voice messages she'd left, she would give up, but that wasn't in her nature.

Once the phone stopped ringing, I noticed once again my mom had left a voice message. With a heavy sigh, I clicked the screen a couple times until my mom's voice rung through my speakers.

"Silas, I do not appreciate you ignoring me and my calls. It's been weeks since you walked out on dinner, and I would think you would have shown your face and apologized by now. Since you refuse to answer my calls, I'll tell you how you can make it up to me. Spencer is due back from Italy next week, and I've arranged for you two to go out. You don't see it now, son, but she would make a wonderful wife and it's about time you start taking your future more serious. I texted you her information, and I'll pass yours along as well. Do not mess this up, Silas. Talk to you later."

Just as the voice message ended, I got a text from my mom. No doubt it was Spencer's number.

Shaking my head, I dropped my phone and tightened my grip on the steering wheel. Talking to my mom was like talking to a brick wall. No matter how many times I shut her down, she kept coming as if I said nothing.

———

When I stepped into my house, I planned on stripping down to my boxers, pouring a drink, and checking to see if I made any money on the games I'd betted on while sitting on my terrace. Sports betting was a hobby I'd taken up a couple years ago, and it'd been a profitable one too.

Since my condo was an open space, I had a full view of the kitchen once I stepped further into my living room, giving me a full view of the beauty moving around.

Biting down on my bottom lip, I raised a brow while seeing Indigo bend over to pick something up. I hadn't seen much of her since the night we slept together. She was normally gone by the time I got home, and when we were here at the same time, she seemed to purposely stay out my way.

"I hear this is your last week," I spoke, causing her to jump and spin around. She looked like she had just got caught with her hand in the cookie jar.

"Mr. Newton." She slapped her hand to her chest. "I thought you would still be working."

Lifting one corner of my mouth, I undid my tie and stepped closer to her. "Since when do you address me by my last name?"

I gave her a once-over, admiring how she looked in the leggings and t-shirt she had on. I licked my lips as memories of the night we spent together popped in my head. I only felt her once, but I wouldn't mind getting between her thighs again. Her locs were pulled back into a low ponytail and face bare of any makeup.

"Sorry, Silas. I'm finishing up now, and I'll be out your hair soon."

I shook my head. "Take your time." I cleared my throat. "So, this is your last week, Fiona told me."

Indigo nodded. "Yes. I finished school, and I'll be starting my new job soon."

I crossed my arms over my chest and cocked my head to the side. "I wasn't aware you were in school."

"Yes. I just finished my master's in chemistry and chemical engineering."

My eyes widened. I wouldn't have expected her to major in something like that. She had been working for me for over a year and I had no idea.

"Impressive." Her cheeks flushed pink.

"Thank you."

Silenced passed by us as she shifted her eyes and crossed her arms in front of her.

My phone went off in my pocket, gaining my attention.

As I took it out and read the text that came through, Indigo spoke again. "Uh Silas." Her voice loud with hesitation.

"Hm?" My eyes never left my phone.

"I'm actually glad I caught you. I needed to speak with you if you have time." That caused me to give her my attention.

"What's going on?"

Whatever was on her mind made her nervous. Part of me wondered if she was tryna ask for the dick again. If I hadn't slept with Ria earlier, I wouldn't have minded.

"C'mon." I nodded for her to follow me over to where my couch was.

The two of us took a seat and I turned to face her. Whatever she was thinking about seemed to be troubling her. You could see the heaviness weighing down on her as she stared at me with a look I couldn't make out.

Typically, I could read people well, but right now I wasn't sure what was going through Indigo's mind. We hadn't had many conversations since we slept together. That night was the most words the two of us shared. I didn't know much about her either, which was obvious since I didn't even know she was in school.

Indigo inhaled a deep breath and when she blew it out a smile formed on her face. It didn't reach her eyes nor was it a happy grin. Just by staring at her it seemed forced as well.

"Indigo?" I called out.

I wondered if she was in trouble and was about to ask for help. Did she want money? Whatever it was, it was starting to cause a bad taste in my mouth.

"Spit it out!" My patience was growing thin.

After inhaling and releasing another deep breath. She folded her hands over her stomach, stared me in the eye, and confessed, "I'm pregnant."

Chapter Five

Indigo

Silas sat still as a rock, staring at me with a look I couldn't decipher. Licking my lips, I drummed my fingers against my thighs while inhaling the *Tom Ford* cologne he wore daily. My stomach was in knots and a lump had formed in the center of my throat.

At first, I wasn't sure how I would break the news to Silas. He was my boss, for one, and we'd only ever had one actual conversation. I could only imagine what was going through his mind at the moment.

My heart was thrashing against my ribcage, ringing in my ears. Time ticked away for what seemed like ages before he finally spoke.

"You're pregnant?" His words came out slowly, laced with confusion.

Nibbling on my bottom lip, I nodded.

He opened his mouth then snapped it closed and scrunched his brows together. "And the reason why you have to tell me is…"

A slight hesitation passed through me, and I cleared my throat. "It's your baby."

Silas' eyes bulged before he rubbed his face with both hands. He dropped them to his knees with a slap.

His shoulder's rolled, and he sat up straighter. "Say that again?" His words now as stiff as his body.

Wetting my now dry lips with my tongue, I repeated my previous statement. My stomach twisted as the hair on my arms and neck raised.

"I know this may be a shock to you, but I—"

"That's impossible." He shut me down before I could finish, dismissing my confession instantly.

"Impossible?" My head cocked back.

Silas cracked his knuckles then stood up and began pacing in front of me. "Yes, impossible." He paused for a moment. "I used a condom. I *always* use a condom."

"It must have broke or something because I *am* pregnant and with *your* baby!"

Silas' eyes cut into tight slits. "It didn't break." He paused and seemed to get lost in thought. "I would have known, and if it did, I would have gotten a Plan B to make sure pregnancy didn't happen. I don't know what you're endgame is but that's not my baby."

My jaw twitched and hands balled up in my lap. Heat flooded my veins, soaring through my body. "It's physically impossible for me to be pregnant by anyone else being you're the only man I've ever had sex with!"

Again, his eyes bucked. "What?" He stepped back from me.

"Shit." I groaned and rubbed my tired eyes. "You heard me. The night we slept together was my first time. I'm three months and if you do the math it adds up. So whether you believe it or not, this *is* your baby."

Tapping my foot, I suddenly felt a wave of exhaustion hit me. I knew there would be resistance from Silas, but I wasn't about to sit here and be called a liar.

Standing up, I ran my clammy hands over my leggings. "Look I know this is a shock to you, but I'm pregnant and this baby is coming. It's inconvenient for me being that I just graduated college and I'm about to start my career. I know you don't know me but pinning a baby on someone isn't in my character. I don't give a damn how much money you're worth, get over yourself." I rolled my eyes.

Whatever nerves I had coming into this conversation were gone. Today was my final day. I promised to stay until Fiona found a replacement and she had, so I was finished here. Silas didn't have to believe me, but this baby was coming either way.

Without waiting for him to say anything else, I went to where my stuff was near the front door. My stomach was growling, and I was exhausted.

Silas didn't try to stop me as I prepared to leave.

I paused for a second before stepping out the door. "We can do a DNA test if you want. I won't be offended." With that I left out, slightly slamming the door behind me.

I rushed down the short hallway to where the elevator was.

Once I got to my car and inside, I took the moment to exhale, feeling my adrenaline finally slow down. The reality of my situation was hitting me, and I had no idea where to go from here.

Hopefully, after a few days, Silas would get his head out his ass and be more open to becoming a parent. If not, I would have to suck it up and do what I needed to do for my baby.

———

"So you're telling me your baby daddy is a millionaire? Bitch, how did you luck up with that?" Audrey gushed with wide eyes.

I waved her off and continued looking through the clothes. Since my weight gain seemed to come rapidly, I was in need of new clothes already. It was annoying being that I pretty much been the same size my whole twenties.

"Audrey, that's irrelevant right now. I don't care about how much money he has. He doesn't even believe this is his baby." I picked a shirt up but then scrunched my nose as I eyed it closer and sat it back down.

We were currently at Nova Rae's Boutique since it wasn't too far from my house. I planned on getting a couple things and since she offered a maternity line now, I decided to give it a try.

"That's minor details. He probably was just in shock. You aren't the type to lie about your baby daddy."

I rolled my eyes and put the jumpsuit I'd just picked up in the shopping bag I had on my arm. "I know that and you know that, but *he* doesn't know that." Shaking my head, I eyed the shopping bag. I had picked out a nice amount that should get me through the next couple weeks. "It doesn't matter anyways. I don't need him."

"Yeah, you're trippin'. Do you know how much that man is worth? He's literally on Forbes' richest young bachelors list, and he's fine as hell."

I pulled my bottom lip between my teeth. That wasn't a lie, Silas was fine as hell. Beyond fine. I would even go as far as to call him gorgeous. With his long, natural lashes and soft, yet masculine features, he could've easily modeled if he wanted.

"Audrey, I don't need you on my back, okay? My parents are already harassing me about the dad and then Charley's ass is so nosy. I don't want to talk about it anymore." Continuing through the store, I picked up a few more things before heading to the wall where the shoes were. I wanted to grab something I would be comfortable in while working.

"Okay just one more thing, Indi, and I'm done. Just don't force yourself to do this alone because we all know you will. Make that man step up whether it's child support or whatever. You didn't make that baby alone."

We headed for the register.

"Hi! Did you find everything okay this evening?" I noticed the name tag and saw it was Nova Rae herself working the register. I had shopped here a few times since moving to Sunset Developments, but this was the first time I caught a glimpse of her.

"I did. I recently found out I'm expecting and love that you have a fashionable maternity line!" Her face lit up.

"Congratulations!" She eyed me. "We'll be dropping more towards the middle of the summer just so you know."

I nodded. "I'll definitely come and check it out."

"I love your store!" Audrey jumped in. "Especially your original collection. I think I buy you out every time you drop a new collection."

Nova Rae smiled at my cousin. "I appreciate that!" She scanned the items from my bag. "The rest of our summer collection will be out the last week of the month."

"I'll be here." Audrey let her know.

I glanced at the accessories on the spin rack on the counter and grabbed a couple earring sets and an anklet then put them on the counter.

Nova Rae finished ringing up my items and I paid and collected my bags.

"Thanks for coming!" We waved to Nova Rae just as a young girl came bouncing from the back.

We left, and the warm air and sunshine hit us. The streets were busy with people and the sounds of cars passing by filled my ears.

"Let's grab food and then have a scary movie marathon." I grinned at my cousin.

She cut her eyes at me. "You know I don't care for scary movies."

I looped my arms through hers. "But you love me." I batted my lashes.

Right now, I didn't feel like being alone. With everything that happened with Silas this week, I found myself feeling vulnerable and slightly needy, which was unlike me.

My cousin rolled her eyes and pushed a dramatic breath out. "Fine."

The corners of my mouth raised. "I knew you loved me."

I had a week until it was time for me to start my new job. I wasn't sure how it would go now that I was pregnant. I knew I couldn't be around chemicals while carrying, but that was an issue I would take on another day.

Chapter Six

Silas

"Are you going to tell me why you called me over here or continue staring into space?" Law asked while studying me carefully.

My attention turned to him, and I cracked my knuckles and rolled my shoulders. "You're the only person I could think of who could help me."

"With what? C'mon, man, this isn't like you. What's up?"

Since Indigo dropped her bomb on me, my mind had been everywhere. I'd barely been able to focus. I kept replaying that night in my head, trying to remember if the condom broke and I didn't realize it. The both of us were pretty fucked-up that night, but I was sure we were safe.

Scrubbing my hands over my face, I flexed my hand. "My maid is accusing me of getting her pregnant."

He stared at me blankly. "Your maid? The one that you been pining over since she was hired?"

I bobbed my head. "That very one."

"Y'all slept together?"

Again, I nodded. "But we used protection."

"Silas, your net worth is in the high millions. Women are going to

41

claim you fathered their kid for that fact alone. Get a DNA test and shut it down."

I shook my head. "I've never had a woman claim I got her pregnant before. I'm *always* careful because I know kids aren't on my agenda. You know me, Law. I'm the most anti-commitment person you could meet. This shit caught me off guard."

Lawson studied me again. "By the way you're acting, I'm guessing you might believe her then."

Standing up, I started pacing the floor. Indigo looked sincere when she told me about her pregnancy. She didn't demand anything of me either, knowing how much I was worth. The fact that she confessed she was a virgin caught me off guard. I remember her having a death grip on me that night and pain flashing through her face, but I just thought it had been a while.

Stopping, I dropped my shoulders forward. "I don't know, man."

"Well, I say get a test done. If it's your baby, step up and be a father." Lawson stood up in front of me. "Being a father is the best thing that could have happened to me, next to marrying Zari. Stop freakin' out."

I frowned. "I'm not tryna be a damn daddy. I like my freedom. And say the baby is mine, then she'll probably expect us to be together. I'm not tryna be tied down by anyone either. I'm not feeling this shit."

Lawson shook his head and crossed his arms over his chest. "Si, Ima be straight up with you. You go around sleeping with multiple women, you were bound to get caught, eventually. You're in your thirties now, it's time to grow up and stop sleeping around anyways. I'm not saying be with your child's mother if the baby is yours but settling down with one woman is better than having a rotation of women."

I shook my head.

I should have known Lawson would come over here and shove being in a relationship down my throat.

When Lawson seen I wasn't going to answer, he grinned. "Look man, my trust was fucked-up before I met Zarinah; hell, even after meeting her." He chuckled. "So, I'm not going to sit here and tell you to take the girl's word. I say meet up with her and set up a test. Find out the results and then go from there. You're the CEO of a huge media company, you can handle possibly having a baby on the way."

The humor in his voice caused my scowl to deepen. "Isn't it time for you to get home to your wife and kid?"

He smirked. "Kicking me out isn't going to make what I said wrong. Handle your business, Silas." His face got serious.

"I hear you."

Meeting up with Indigo was needed. The last thing I needed was her going around claiming I fathered her kid. If that news got out and the news picked it up, it could cause a media frenzy for me.

Lawson stayed around for a little longer before heading out.

The moment I was alone, I went to my couch and plopped down. My muscles were tight and my temples pounded.

Instead of dwelling in my thoughts and driving myself crazy, I got up and went to my bar to pour me a cold one then to my study where I logged into my online poker account. Gambling was one thing that always relaxed me.

Bringing my glass to my mouth, I took a drink while getting lost in the game. I wasn't sure how many hours had gone by before my focus was broken by my phone going off. Right now, I was currently even and it was almost time to show our hands.

When I glanced at my phone, I noticed a number that wasn't saved had texted me. Picking my phone up, I inwardly groaned after seeing it was Spencer. This was the first time she had reached out to me since our mothers decided to give our numbers to one another. She was asking to meet up when she got back into town.

Unmoving, my eyes shifted when my computer dinged from the game still going on. Knowing how hard my mom was going to go hook me up with someone was nerve wrecking and irritating as hell.

I didn't respond right away. Instead, I locked my phone back and went back to my game. Right now I had money to win, and that was the only thing that owned my attention at the moment.

———

Indigo opened her door and stepped back, allowing me in her house.

"We can talk in here. Do you want something to drink or anything?" she asked, turning and heading towards her couch.

"Nah, I'm good." I followed behind her.

After a few days of going over what Lawson said, I decided he was right. I needed to man-up and talk to Indigo about this whole baby thing so I could move on. Since I didn't have her number, Fiona was shocked when I asked her to reach out to Indigo being that she didn't work for me anymore. I didn't go into details outside of I needed to speak with her.

Adjusting my body so I was facing her, I ran my eyes over her. I noticed the obvious changes on her body easily. In the tank top she wore it was hard to miss the roundness in her stomach or fullness of her breast.

"So, you wanted to talk?" She picked up a bottle on the table next to her and brought it to her mouth.

I nodded. "You claim I'm the father of your kid."

Indigo lowered the bottle and narrowed her eyes while pressing her lips together. "And while I still say it's not true, I would rather be positive so we can both move on."

Indigo's eyes peered into me like lasers, and she didn't speak right away. I took the moment to look around her house. It was decorated in yellow, gray, and white. Pictures of her with family and friends scattered around the living room. In the pictures, she looked happy. and in each one she held a genuine smile or silly face with whoever was in it.

"So, you want a DNA test? And when it comes back that you are the father then what?" She cocked her head to the side. Her voice stoic.

"Then, we work something out."

"Meaning what exactly? I don't know what you think this is, Silas, but having a baby isn't a game. When you find out this is your baby, are you going to be there? Do you think you're just going to throw money at it and not be present because if that's the case then keep it, I won't accept a half-ass daddy in my baby's life. I don't care who or how much money you have."

Sadly, the sass in her voice made my dick twitch in the khaki shorts I was wearing. Indigo came off as quiet, but I could tell she had some fire to her. "If it turns out the baby is mine, I plan on being there. *Physically* that is, but we'll cross that bridge when we get there."

She brought her bottom lip between her teeth and nodded. "Okay. I'll talk to my doctor at my next appointment and ask."

"When is that? The appointment?"

"In two weeks. It'll be my four-month checkup." My eyes bucked.

I glanced down at her stomach. Vaguely, I remember her mentioning how far along she was when she told me she was pregnant. "You're only three months."

Her mouth turned upside down. "What does that mean?"

I ran my hand over the top of my head, then grabbed the back of my neck. "Uh nothing, I didn't expect you to be that far, I guess."

She cleared her throat. "You're free to come to my appointment if you want, that way we can talk to my doctor about the test and you can ask any other questions you have."

Her calmness was throwing me off. I had never been in this position before, but I didn't think most women would be this relaxed in this situation.

"Why are you so calm?" I raised an eyebrow.

"Why wouldn't I be?" She scrunched her face up and shifted her body.

"I mean most women would be upset if a guy asked for a DNA test, right?" I scratched my chin. "You're taking all this well."

Indigo shrugged. "Because I don't blame you for having doubts. You don't know me and I'm sure this isn't something new for you. Contrary to what you might think, I'm not out for your money. I wasn't planning on getting pregnant either, it just happened. You wanting a test doesn't shock me, in fact, I would be shocked if you didn't ask for one." She took a drink out her bottle again.

I roamed my eyes over her.

"Send Fiona your appointment information, and I'll try and make it. I probably don't have to say this, but until we get this straightened out, I would rather keep this under wraps. I don't want the news getting wind of this and causing a scandal."

I also didn't want my mother getting wind of this.

A shiver shot through me at the thought. I could only imagine how that whole conversation would go.

"Trust me, you have nothing to worry about. I just want to continue my quiet little life with no issues."

"Glad we're on the same page."

I stood up and prepared to leave.

"I'll talk to you later." She opened the door.

Taking the moment to look at her, I zeroed in on her stomach. It was a nice size to it. Being around pregnant women wasn't my specialty but if she was already showing this much this early, I could only imagine how big she would be the further she got.

Lifting my eyes to her face, she seemed to be watching me while holding onto the door. Her locs were pulled half up with two out in the front over her forehead.

Normally, I wouldn't look twice at a female with locs, but they looked good on her.

Nodding at her, I walked out her house and headed for my car.

Taking my phone out my pocket, I went to Fiona's name and clicked on it. The moment she answered, I didn't give her a chance to speak.

"I need a full background check on Indigo on my desk first thing in the morning."

Chapter Seven

Indigo

"I'm sorry about this," I apologized as I followed behind the director of the clinic I would be working for. He was currently giving me the tour of the building. I had just finished my onboarding paperwork and was excited to see the work site.

My mentor had set me up with healthcare clinic in the valley, in Butter Ridge Falls, which is considered the more industrial part of town. The part of the clinic I would be working at focused on genetic testing and gene therapy.

Starting a new job, especially being freshly out of college and pregnant, wasn't ideal.

"No need to apologize. Dr. Robinson had nothing but great things to say about you when she recommended you. I was also impressed during your interview. We don't discriminate here."

"I know, but I just want you to know I didn't plan on starting the job while pregnant. I promise it won't affect my work ethic."

He glanced over his shoulder at me, giving me a slight nod. "I'm sure it won't. Of course, we'll have to work around what you can be around for the time being while you're carrying, however."

My hand went to my stomach.

My biggest setback would be the hazard chemicals the lab called for when it came to the tests we had to conduct. Even with the mask and suits we wore, I wasn't sure if it was safe to be around them while pregnant. Still, I planned on taking every step I could to be able to stay in the lab and keep my baby safe until I could no longer do so.

Dr. Foe continued showing me around the clinic, introducing me to the different workers and scientists I would be working with. For the most part, everyone seemed welcoming. There were a few women in the field, but most were men, which was to be expected. One thing I loved about choosing this profession was that I was the underdog. Not a lot of women took this route and excelled at it. I loved beating the odds.

"That's all for today. Do you have any questions?" Dr. Foe asked once we were back in front of the conference room we started at.

I shook my head.

I felt like I was floating right now. For so long, I imagined being in this positioned. All I ever wanted to do was work in a lab and now it was becoming a reality. I couldn't wait to officially start.

"No. I'm good."

He nodded. "Good. Don't be afraid to speak up if something doesn't make sense. I know starting off things can seem intimidating but I saw your marks, and you're a bright woman. I have no doubt you'll fit it fine here."

It took everything in me not to fan girl right now. Dr. Foe was a fine-looking older man. He had to be mid-forties, possibly early fifties. He sported some salt and pepper in his low-cut hair and short goatee. His skin reminded me of cinnamon. My eyes went to his left hand. I didn't see a ring, so I was assuming he wasn't married either.

"I have no doubt about that." I grinned.

"Dr. Foe, we need you in room three." A younger guy approached us.

Dr. Foe looked over his shoulder. "Yes. Here I come." He looked back at me. "I have to go. I'll see you here tomorrow first thing in the morning for your first official day." He held his hand out."

Happily, I grabbed it and shook it.

Dr. Foe was my ideal guy; he was older, mature, smart, and if I wasn't carrying someone else's baby and he wasn't my boss, I would've shoot my shot at him.

Sighing, I shook my head; a girl could dream.

I headed out towards the entrance of the clinic where the lobby was located. In the front, an urgent care was ran here for a limited part of the day.

When I got to my car, I couldn't help my grimace as I glanced down. I felt like each time I glanced at my stomach it only got bigger. Everyone was telling me it was in my head, but I knew I wasn't crazy.

Taking one more look at the brick building, I climbed inside my car and started it up, instantly rolling down my windows.

I was happy that being pregnant didn't hinder my job, and I was excited to show my skills as a scientist.

———

To say I was shocked to see that Silas showed up to my appointment was an understatement. When I reached out to confirm if he was coming, he told me he wasn't going to be able to make it and Fiona was going to come in his place.

I couldn't lie and say I wasn't disappointed. When I saw him walk into my doctor's office, I was surprised.

"I thought you weren't going to make it?" I side-eyed him while looking around the examination room.

"I didn't think I would either, but my meetings ended sooner than I expected." He loosened his tie.

Silas rubbed his jaw and gazed at me. "What's supposed to happen today, exactly?"

I shrugged. "This is the first time I'll be seeing my actual doctor. I'm assuming they'll go over my bloodwork, do an ultrasound, confirm my due date."

He frowned. "What do you mean the first time you've seen your doctor. How did you know how far along you are if you haven't seen a doctor?"

"I *have* seen a doctor." I rolled my eyes. "At the hospital. "I passed out at my graduation because I was dehydrated and exhausted. I learned I was pregnant that same day."

His phone went off, gaining his attention. When he glanced at the screen, the muscle in his jaw ticked and eyes tightened. He tapped his screen a few times, completely getting lost in whoever had texted him.

After a few seconds, a small chuckle left his mouth.

My fingers drummed along my thigh. It was odd being alone with Silas because I didn't know anything about him. I didn't know how to act around him or how he would react to certain things. He still didn't believe he fathered my child, and the only reason he was here was to get information about a DNA test. The whole situation was draining, honestly.

A knock on the door had gained both our attention. My doctor, Dr. Hill, who had been my OB since I was a teenager, walked in the room.

"Indigo. I was not expecting to see you anytime soon. Congratulations are in order." I gave her a bashful smile.

"Hi, Dr. Hill."

She stepped into the room and over to the sink to wash her hands. Once she was finished, she turned and paused, then her eyes widened. "Oh, I didn't realize someone was with you. You must be Dad."

Her eyes zeroed in on Silas, who stayed quiet.

I rolled my eyes. "Yes, he is."

Dr. Hill cleared her throat. "Okay then. I looked over your bloodwork and everything looks good. Your iron is still a little low, which I gather they told you at the hospital. Besides that, it all looked good. How about we give a listen?"

I nodded when she approached me. "Did you have any concerns about anything?" Dr. Hill questioned while she listened to my heart.

"No. Everything's been going fine. Well, there is one thing." While I was talking, my eyes stayed locked on Silas. He was watching Dr. Hill examine me but hadn't spoken a word since she walked in the room.

"I feel huge. Like I know you gain weight while pregnant, but I'm too early to be this big, right?"

Dr. Hill stepped away from me and looked me over. "Everyone is different when it comes to how they carry. Some gain weight early and some late. Nothing about your gaining is alarming to me, however. Your heart and lungs sound good." She moved to my stomach.

Dr. Hill continued her examination and then got me set up for my ultrasound.

Silas was still quiet during everything. I would have forgotten he was there if it wasn't for his phone periodically going off. When it came time for my ultrasound, he moved the chair he was sitting on a little closer to where I was to get a closer view.

The disconnect between us couldn't be any clearer. It made me feel some type of way. If he wasn't going to engage in any way, he could have waited in the lobby until Dr. Hill was finished.

A shiver shot through me when the cool gel hit my stomach. My heart pounded loudly and my blood hummed through my veins in anticipation of seeing my baby.

"Okay, let's hear the heartbeat first." Dr. Hill tapped the machine a few times and placed the doppler on my stomach.

When the heartbeat started, I became alert. It didn't sound the same as it did when I was at the hospital.

"Why does it sound like that?" I asked in a panic.

My chest tightened as I rose slightly off the examination table.

"Something's wrong?" Silas' deep baritone sounded for the first time. I glanced at him and he had a hardened expression on his face as he stared at the monitor.

I swallowed hard.

"No, no. Just hold on." Dr. Hill assured me.

She tapped a few buttons, and the monitor lit up with a black and white image. "Okay, you see there." She pointed at the screen. "Looks like you two got a two-for-one special."

My brows shot up in surprise. "What?"

"See." She pointed. "Two embryos. One sac. Identical twins."

My tongue suddenly became tied as shock flew threw me. Whipping my head over to Silas, I was sure our faces matched.

"Twins? You never said you were having twins."

I shook my head. "I didn't know. The hospital didn't tell me that."

"Well, it looks like Twin B could have been hiding behind Twin A. He or she is a little smaller. Both look good, however." She hit a few buttons and the machine started printing.

Wordlessly, I stared at her while processing what she was saying. There was no way I was about to have two kids.

"I, no, I—" I stuttered. Inhaling a sharp breath, I took a second to gather myself. "I'm having twins. Like two babies?"

Dr. Hill nodded. "Yes, you are. It's too early to tell the sex, but it explains why you feel like you're gaining weight at a rapid rate. When you carry multiples, you typically grow faster."

Once Dr. Hill wiped my stomach off and I sat up. She handed me the printouts of my sonogram.

"At the moment, I have no concerns. The further you get along, we might want to revisit some things. Everyone handles pregnancy differently but carrying more than one can take a toll on some women so I want to be safe rather than sorry. Any questions?" Her eyes bounced between us.

"Are we able to get a DNA test while she's pregnant?" A shocked expression appeared on the doctor's face. I had forgotten that was the whole reason Silas had come today. Heat rushed to my cheeks.

"Uhm." She cleared her throat and gave me a questioning look. "A paternity test can be given while pregnant, however, there is a small risk to the fetus; in this case, fetuses and mother."

I pressed my lips together, and my stomach turned.

"Can we set it up?" I whipped my head to face Silas. My eyes narrowed at him.

"Indigo, is that what you want?" My chest clenched and blood ran cold. It was like he had disregarded what she had just said without a second thought.

Slowly dragging my eyes back to my doctor, I nodded. "Yes. I would like to set it up." I could see the apprehension on her face.

"Are you sure?"

Slowly, I bobbed my head. "Yes."

The sooner I got this over with the better. At first, I wanted the test because I wanted to show I wasn't lying, now I wanted it to rub it in

Silas' face. The more I was around him the more I saw how much of an asshole he could be.

"Good. Let's set that up, ASAP." He took his phone out and started tapping the screen.

I bit down on the inside of my cheek, forcing myself not to react to his rudeness.

It took another ten minutes for us to set up the DNA test and my next appointment then we were leaving out the appointment.

I noticed Silas was parked near me once we got outside. Before we got in our cars, I turned to look at him.

"You know, you could have taken into consideration that she said there was a risk to me and the babies before you demanded the test." My hand went to my hip and mouth pouted.

He stared at me with a stern expression. His brows pulled tightly together.

"I need to know if you're carrying my children or not. I'm sure if it was a large risk, she wouldn't have mentioned it."

My mouth dropped. "You're serious."

"You could be carrying the next generation of Newtons, that's something I need to know now rather than later."

My eyes narrowed and nostrils flared. "You know what, I'm going to do the test just because I don't want any doubt about my kids' dad, but as far as them being the next generation of Newtons, fuck you!"

I turned and snatched my door open and climbed inside my car, slamming the door shut behind me.

I didn't bother giving Silas a second glance. Quickly, I started my car and skirted out the parking lot. The nerve of him being so inconsiderate of me and my kids' wellbeing.

———

"Twins?" Both my parents' brows shot up. My mom's damn near touched her hairline. With a tight smile, I nodded and handed them each a sonogram.

Internally, I was freaking out and I needed someone to reel me in. I loved my cousin and sister, but they weren't who I needed for the job right now. I knew my parents would be the ones to talk me off the edge. A lot was happening right now. I'd started at the clinic and loved it so far. Dr. Foe was a great boss and patient. I worked alongside him at first and felt like I learned so much before he passed me to the senior scientist. Surprisingly, she was a female and a hard ass, but I was never the one to be intimidated easily.

"Wow." My mom's eyes shot to mine. "Twins…twins!" Her voice elevated and face lit up. "I was excited about having one grandchild, but now two."

"Identical ones too," I threw in there.

My mom clapped her hands. "This is the best news. Babies and pregnancy are a beautiful thing. If I was able to, I would have had at least ten kids."

My dad's head cocked to the side and whipped to face my mom. "Ten?"

She smacked her lips. "Yes, Noah. You know I wanted a big family. Three wasn't enough." She waved my dad off.

His brows dipped into a frown. Shaking his head, he turned to face me.

"How do you feel about this, Indi? One baby is one thing, but two is a lot to handle."

Bringing the corner of my bottom lip between my teeth, I gnawed on it for a second and felt small flutters form in my stomach. I knew it was too soon for the babies to be moving, at least I thought it was, so I chalked it up to butterflies.

"I'm scared," I admitted.

I'd always had an open relationship with my parents. Being the oldest, I was always the one who felt like I had to carry everything on my back. I always made sure to look out for my younger siblings. Even though me and my sister were closer than me and my brother, I loved both of them. While my siblings were a little more carefree, I always made sure to keep some kind of structure.

"Oh, sweetheart." Sympathy filled my mom's face.

"I'm excited, don't get me wrong. I mean, I wasn't expecting to have kids or anything right now, but now that's it happening, I can't stop it. Learning it's not one but two kids was shocking for me. Not to mention the dad..." My voice faded away and my eyes shifted.

"The dad what?" My dad sat up straighter.

"Does he know?" my mom questioned.

I wet my lips and nodded. "Yes, he does. He was there today when we found out about the twins."

"And is he excited?"

I pictured Silas. From the moment I told him about being pregnant, he wasn't on board with it. He questioned everything and came off standoffish. Today, him disregarding the health of me and our kids showed he really didn't care like I hoped he would.

"He doesn't believe they're his." I winced as I spoke.

"What?"

"Why would he feel like that?"

Their voice mixed as they stared at me.

I shook my head. "I don't blame him. I mean not really. We're not in a relationship or anything. Actually, he was my boss."

"And he took advantage of you?" My dad gritted.

Quickly, I shook my head with wide eyes. "No! No he didn't! It was consensual on both ends, but like I said we weren't in a relationship and it was one night. I don't blame him. I agreed to a DNA test. I just hope once it comes back that he is the father, he'll have a change of heart."

My parents shared a look. "And who is he, Indi? Is it someone we know?" My mom asked.

Again, I nibbled the corner of my bottom lip and shook my head. "His name is Silas. Silas Newton."

"Silas Newton," my dad whispered. His eyes grew. "The CEO of that media firm, what's its name?" He snapped his fingers a couple times. "Culture Ties Media! I just saw an interview about him a couple days ago on TV."

I bobbed my head. "That's him. He's who I been working for."

"Shit." My dad ran his hand over his head. "That's one of the biggest names in the media right now."

"I know," I groaned.

Once learning I was pregnant, I went and did my research on Silas. I knew a little about him from working with him, but nothing serious. From what I gathered, he was seen around a lot with different model looking girls, he came from a wealthy family, he built his company from the ground up with money he got from an inheritance, and he'd been behind a lot of popular outlets' success.

"Can someone fill me in?" My mom scrunched her nose up.

My dad looked at her with a blank look. He grabbed his phone and hit the screen a few times before handing it over to her.

"So, if I'm guessing, he thinks you're trying to get money or something from him?"

My shoulders rose. "I can only assume."

My mom scuffed. "Oh please. I mean he's a handsome man and yes he's loaded, but you aren't the type of girl to try and trap a man for money." She thrusted my dad's phone back.

"Well, of course not. We didn't raise a damn gold digger and if that young man believes otherwise, I'll have a conversation with him myself." My dad sat up straight, and his face hardened.

"Okay, both of you chill!" I tossed both my hands up. My heart warmed knowing how hard my parents went for me. No matter how old I was, I knew I could depend on them. "I don't want any harm to come to him." I narrowed my eyes at my dad and he threw the same look back at me. "I'm holding on to hope that he'll come around after the test."

"And if he doesn't?" My mom raised a brow.

I shrugged. "Then, we'll go from there." My parents shared a look again. They always had a way to communicate without communicating out loud.

I inhaled a deep breath. "I don't want to think about all that right now. Right now, I'm just trying to comprehend the fact that I'll be the mother of two. I'm nervous."

"You're going to be a great mother, Indi. You don't have to worry about that," my mom assured.

"You sure are. Those babies are gonna be lucky to have you as their mother."

A smile found its way onto my face. I knew I would have the support of my family. They never had been the ones to let me down.

Both of my parents were successful lawyers. My mom was in family law and my dad was in corporate law. Even with their busy schedules, they were always there for me and my siblings. We weren't rich like Silas and his family, but they made good money that put us in the higher middle class. They made sure we never went without and always made sure at least one of them were home to tell us goodnight every night when we were younger.

They were the model parents, the ones I aimed to be like. If I could be half the parent my mom and dad were, I knew my babies would be just fine.

Chapter Eight

Silas

I ndigo and I walked silently out the building where her doctor had just performed the DNA test. Since setting the test up, we hadn't had much communication, and today when we showed up at the doctor's office, she was quiet.

I had chosen to have my car service pick her up today and drive the both of us. The moment she got in the car, I could tell she wasn't feeling the procedure, and I almost backed out of it, but I needed to know. Waiting until the babies were born was too long. Indigo still had months left of her pregnancy, and if these were my kids she was carrying, the sooner I had it confirmed the better. I hadn't said anything to anyone outside of Fiona and Lawson. I especially made sure my parents didn't find out until the test came back. The last thing I needed was for my mom to interfere.

"Are you hungry or do you need anything?" I asked once we were in the car. There were a few things I needed to handle today that I'd put off until this evening.

Indigo shook her head and rubbed her stomach. My eyes dropped. "Are you in pain?"

Dr. Hill warned us there could be minor side effects which included

58

cramping. Indigo was far enough in her pregnancy that the risk for miscarriage was minimum.

Indigo had a vacant look on her face. She lifted her head and looked out the window. Her face balled up. "Where are we going? This isn't the way to my house."

"I'm taking you to the office with me." I pulled out my phone to reply to a few texts.

"Why would you do that?" Her face scrunched more.

"Because the doctor said you need to be on the lookout for cramping and bleeding and all that. If it happens you shouldn't be alone."

Her eyes cut into slits and mouth pinched together. "So now you care about that?" Her arms crossed over her ample chest. She turned her mouth upside down.

"Look, maybe I didn't handle things well at first. I should have taken your feelings into consideration more, but the test is done now. All that's left to do is wait for the results. I'll keep an eye on you for the rest of the day to make sure you're good and then you can go home tomorrow."

"Tomorrow?"

I nodded and went back to my phone. "It only makes sense that you stay overnight so you can be monitored."

"I have work tomorrow."

"You can still go to work."

I tapped the phone. "I work in Butter Ridge Falls."

"That's what cars are for."

Fiona had forwarded me a couple forms that needed my signature. I also noticed a text had come through from my mom, which I didn't hesitate to clear. I knew she was only reaching out because I hadn't made solid plans with Spencer.

"You can't just dictate my life and make plans. What if I had some-thing to do after this." Glancing up, I noticed an annoyed look was now on her face. She rubbed her stomach. Her face slightly winced.

"That look right there is the reason why you don't need to be alone. Last week you were complaining I didn't give a damn about your health. Now I'm trying to care and you're still upset. Pick a feeling." I went back to my phone.

"You're being selfish, that's my issue. You don't care about how I feel! All you care about is yourself." My jaw ticked while her stomach grumbled.

"Figure out what you want to eat, and I'll have Fiona have it brought to the office," I let her know.

"What? Did you just hear what I said?"

I ignored her.

Maybe my actions were selfish, but they were justified. She was worried before the procedure, so I was gonna keep an eye on her. I needed to be in the office so that's where she would be too, regardless of what she was saying right now.

———

The workday was ending, and I had just finished up my last phone call for the day when a knock on the door gained my attention.

"Come in."

Fiona stepped inside with her iPad in her arms. "Busy day today," she commented.

Sighing, I slacked back in my chair. "You can say that again." I yawned.

I had been on the go since Indigo's appointment. The moment I got to the office, I was busy with phone calls and a meeting with the head of operations. Of few of the clients under us weren't projecting the numbers we hoped with their current marketing plan and there was concern. I tried to be as hands-on with our clients as I could. We were a large firm and a lot of companies put their faith in us to make their business grow. So once a week, I made sure to figure out which businesses under us weren't doing well and determine how to change it. We also had just picked up a big client that wanted to create a new social media reading app of some sorts. That was my last call today, finalizing the details before the contracts got involved.

"Looks like she did too." Her eyes traveled to the couch on the right where Indigo was currently sleeping, peacefully.

"Yeah well according to her, being pregnant with two babies drains a lot of energy."

Indigo still didn't say much once we got to my firm. It was in the center of downtown New Haven and my office was on the top floor. I watched as she admired the place, but she didn't ask any questions.

The moment we got to my office, she went to the couch and got on her phone. The food Fiona had ordered was delivered shortly after.

"She's a nice girl, you know. The moment I hired her I took a liking to her." My eyes went my back to my assistant.

Fiona had become like family over the years, and I took her opinion serious in most cases. If it wasn't for her, my life wouldn't run nearly as smooth as it did.

"I'm sure she is."

I began shutting down for the night.

"And I don't believe she's the type to pin a baby on anyone. We've talked a lot over the year she's worked for you. She's a smart girl, very ambitious. All she wanted was to graduate school and be in a science lab somewhere."

My brows furrowed. "What are you telling me all this for?"

A sly grin formed on her face and her shoulders lifted. "Just that it wouldn't hurt to be a little more open at you being the father of her kids."

"I have her here in my office right now. What more do you want me to do?" My face slacked as I stared at her.

Fiona rolled her eyes. "Maybe, I don't know, try and be a little gentler with her."

"Gentler?" My eyes squinted and head turned so I could give Indigo a once-over. "You act like I'm beating on her or something." Indigo shifted in her sleep and mumbled something inaudible while her hands rested on her stomach.

"No, but you're not being considerate of how she feels either."

Fiona and Indigo were in my office alone while I handled some things in one of my conference rooms. Now I was wondering what the two of them discussed while I was gone.

"Call the car and have them meet us downstairs. I'm done here for the day," I let her know, no longer wanting to discuss this.

"Silas—"

"Fiona, you out of everyone know I don't like being forced into anything. Once the test is back, we'll revisit how I handle Indigo. As for now, how things are going is fine. Now the car." My voice was stern, and I kept gathering my things to leave.

Fiona muttered under breath but did as I requested.

It didn't take a long time for me to shut down my office and stand to leave. "She looks so peaceful," Fiona spoke behind me as I stood above Indigo.

She did look peaceful with her mouth slightly parted. Small snores came from her. She slept as if she had no worries in the world.

I shook my head and bent down. "You can go now, Fiona. Indigo." My hand went to her shoulder, giving it a slight shake.

She grumbled and went to brush my hand away. "Indigo." My voice was a little louder.

Her eyes fluttered and a pout formed on her face. "What?"

"C'mon. The car is here and it's time to leave."

Confusion filled her face for a second as she slowly arose and looked around. Apparently, she had forgotten she was in my office.

"Oh, yeah okay." She yawned. Reaching in her lap, she picked her phone up and looked at the screen.

Once she was fully up and standing, we headed for the door. My office was the only one on this floor and my secretary was gone for the day.

"God, I'm starving," Indigo complained, rubbing her stomach.

"You just ate a few hours ago."

She frowned and glared at me while we waited for the elevator. "I am eating for three now and it's been like three hours!"

Dropping my attention to her forming stomach, I slowly trekked my eyes up, pausing at her breast and moving back to her face.

"We can stop and grab you something to eat on the way."

"I can just cook when we get to your house." We stepped on the elevator once it arrived.

"Yeah, I doubt I have anything there to cook. Most of the time I get meal prepped meals delivered every week, and when I don't want to eat those, I eat out because I'm hardly home."

"Wow, must be nice," she muttered and scrolled through her phone.

"So, decide what you want and we can grab it."

Pausing, she glanced up at me. "You're serious about me coming home with you?"

I nodded and looked up, watching the numbers highlight as we passed the floors. "I wouldn't have said it if I wasn't. How are you feeling?"

"I'm fine." She shifted her eyes away from me.

I couldn't tell if she was telling the truth, but Indigo didn't come off as the type not to speak up if something was wrong with her.

When we got to the main lobby, it was empty. I was typically the last person to leave the building most days so it didn't surprise me.

The car service I used sometimes was waiting for us outside.

The moment we were inside, I didn't hesitate to undo my tie, set my briefcase down, and lean back in my seat with my eyes closed.

"Did you always want to do the kind of work you do?" Indigo's voice broke through the silence of the car.

When I used my car service, I typically wanted to ride home in silence so I could unwind for the day.

Opening my eyes, I turned to look at her for a second. "Basically. I've always had fun with marketing and all that, but I wanted to go a step beyond that."

Grabbing my phone, I saw I had a notification from my latest sports bet. I went through my earnings. This week, I'd lost more than I gained.

"I know the feelings." She yawned.

"You're a scientist, right?" I questioned, keeping my eyes on the phone. I was preparing my next round of bets.

"I am." Her face beamed. "I just graduated with my master's in chemistry and chemical engineering."

I knew that from the background check, but still it surprised me that she was in a challenging field. I hated science and math.

"You must be smart to get a degree in both of those." Out the corner of my eyes, I saw her shoulders rise then fall.

"I am."

"Then, why work as a maid?" This time, I gave her my attention.

"I needed the money for school. I didn't want to do any loans or rely on my parents, and my scholarships only covered so much."

I studied Indigo for a moment. "That's honorable."

Her smile grew, but I could see the exhaustion in her eyes. "Yeah, I guess. It wasn't ideal but I made it happen. Now I'm doing what I love with minimal debt."

My phone dinged and when I looked, I saw it was my mom again. Sighing, I weighed my options. I knew if I kept blowing her off, she would make her presence known rather I wanted to or not.

Making a mental note to call her when I got home, I turned to Indigo to see what she wanted to eat. It wouldn't be long before we were at my house.

"Wow." I stared at her in amusement. That quickly she had fallen asleep. Her head leaned back and those small snores from when she slept at my office had returned.

Deciding to let her sleep, I bent down to go into my briefcase when a weight on my shoulder gained my attention.

Indigo's head had shifted, and she was now peacefully sleeping on my shoulder.

A small grin tugged on my face. She looked younger when she was sleeping. Her nose slightly flared as she breathed softly.

I brushed one of her locs out her face to get a clearer view. Her face had started gaining a little weight, I assumed because of the pregnancy. Whatever she used in her hair to maintain her locs filled my nose, sending something I couldn't name through me.

Thankfully, she hadn't complained about any discomfort since leaving the test earlier. The last thing I wanted was complications to flare up. My thoughts on everything were a little selfish like she mentioned, but I couldn't help it. Growing up and having every choice made for you made it hard to be lenient as an adult.

Fiona's words played in my head. Maybe I was being a little too cold with Indigo. She seemed harmless enough.

Instead of disturbing her, I adjusted some and leaned my head back, closing my eyes.

Chapter Nine

Indigo

"How are you feeling after being here for two weeks?" Dr. Foe asked as we finished up the day.

With a smile on my face, I turned to look at him. "I love it. It doesn't even feel like I'm working half the time."

He placed a few beakers on the metal rack in front of him.

"You catch on quick. The kind of work we do here is important to the future of medicine and people. It's not easy what we do, but you're holding your own and have become a great asset to the team."

I beamed brightly. "I appreciate that. Science has always been my first love."

He nodded. "You can tell. You're dedicated and talented. I can see you going far."

My head lowered to hide my blush. "Thank you, sir."

I opened the fridge and placed a few chemicals inside. I had to be careful with certain things I handled since I was pregnant, and so far it hadn't been an issue. Today, we were handling some genetic testing, which had me curious about my pregnancy going forward. As far as I knew, my family was healthy and I didn't have a lot to worry about, but I didn't know a lot about Silas or his family history. My doctor hadn't mentioned anything wrong with my babies but after working in the lab these past couple of weeks and seeing some of the things we'd discovered, it had me curious.

A yawn escaped my mouth, and I rubbed my eyes. "Tired?" He eyed me.

I shook my head. "No, I'm fine. Just the day catching up with me."

I went back to work station and grabbed a few more things that needed to go in the fridge.

"You know I admire you, Indigo. Even though you came highly recommended, learning you were pregnant had me a bit worried, but the more I work with you the more I see I have nothing to worry about it."

The more compliments Dr. Foe showered me with, the warmer my body grew. I normally wasn't the one who needed my ego stroked or praised for the work I did because I was naturally a hard worker but hearing it from someone like Dr. Foe was different. He knew his stuff and was good at his job. He had worked with a lot of different clinical trials to help different diseases, and he was a great teacher and someone I looked up to.

"You don't have to worry about anything. Being pregnant isn't going to slow me down. If anything, it'll only cause me to work harder."

For a second, his eyes dropped to my stomach then snapped back to me. "I have no doubt about that."

Grinning harder, I quickly turned around when I felt heat rush to my cheeks. I always enjoyed working with Dr. Foe, personally. Tonight it was just the two of us shutting things down and even though I didn't mind the rest of the team, working directly with the boss was always better.

We continued cleaning up and shutting the lab down and by the time we were done, all I wanted to do was eat, shower, and go to bed.

"Great work today, Indigo. I'll see you tomorrow," Dr. Foe commented, holding my car door open.

"Thank you, Dr. Foe."

"Please call me Greg outside the lab." Hearing that made heat rush to the tip of my ears and my heart stutter.

I bit back a smile and batted my lashes. "Greg. Thank you."

I climbed inside the car. My stomach had grown the past couple weeks and the twins weren't being shy about being seen.

On my way home, I stopped around the corner from my house and grabbed me a mango passion fruit tea from Java Books.

I didn't have to worry about getting food because surprisingly, Silas's chef had meal prepped me food and he had it delivered to me. I had mentioned to Fiona in passing how it was a nuisance to cook when I got off work now because I found myself wanting to curl up in bed. She mentioned it to Silas and proclaimed he insisted on having his chef make meals for me. I wasn't sure if I believed her or not, but I was thankful. I didn't have to cook this week unless I was craving something particular.

Sitting on my couch, I was going through my mail and my stomach knotted after seeing the name of the testing center that did the DNA test. It had been a week since we did the test and me and Silas hadn't been in communication like that, outside of a few texts. I mainly spoke with Fiona. I wouldn't call us friends, but she was easier to talk to than her boss.

Since I knew what the results would be, I wasn't sure why I was nervous to open them. My biggest concern was how Silas would act knowing that he was indeed the father of my kids. Hopefully, his attitude towards everything would change and he would be more open to everything.

I wet my lips and tapped the envelope on my thigh.

My phone vibrated on my coffee table and when I looked at it, I was surprised to see Silas was not only calling but Facetiming me.

Gnawing on my bottom lip, the knot in my stomach grew tighter. We didn't talk on the phone let alone Facetime.

Reaching and grabbing the phone, I hit the green button and waited for the call to connect. A few seconds later, Silas' face appeared on the screen. It looked as if he had just gotten home from the office and was still in his suit. His hair looked freshly lined up.

"The results came," he started the conversation. No hello, no how are you, straight to business.

Instead of speaking, I nodded my head. His face was set in a hard, blank expression. I wasn't sure how he was feeling seeing the proof he needed in black and white.

"Did you receive them as well?" Again, I nodded my head.

A dark, sickening grief filled my heart. Silas didn't seem as if he was on board with being a parent. His eyes were vacant of whatever he was feeling and his face stilled.

My other hand went to my stomach. The ticks of my heart passed through us while silence filled the air.

Silas cleared his throat. "It seems you were right. I am the father of your twins." His answer was smug. Blinking a few times, I squinted my eyes waiting for him to continue.

"Now that we have confirmation, we can proceed forward."

"Proceed forward?" My brows drew closer.

"There are certain expectations now that we know you're carrying a Newton. Now that we know you're carrying my legacy, things are a little more complicated on my end, but I'll handle that. The babies and you, of course, will be taken care of going forward. I'll have accounts set up and—"

I wasn't sure what he meant by that, but I needed to say a few things before he continued. He was acting like we were speaking business instead of about our kids.

"Silas!" I blurted out.

My head was spinning. He went from not believing he was the father of my kids to setting up accounts. Things were moving too fast. His brows furrowed. "I believe we need to sit down and talk face-to-face. Obviously, things are going to change for the both of us and I would like for us to be on the same page with things."

With a stiff nod, he agreed. "I'll send my car service to pick you up Friday evening at eight. The chef will prepare us something to eat and we'll have dinner here at the house."

My mouth parted to speak but he kept talking. "Since it'll be late, I suggest you pack a bag so you can stay the night. Let Fiona know what you want to eat. We it can be prepared by the time you arrive."

"Silas."

"I have another call. I'll see you Friday." He ended the call before I could say another word.

With my mouth ajar, I blinked slowly staring at my phone. One thing I was learning about Silas is he was controlling. He didn't leave much room to go against what he had to say, which was something I had to address at dinner.

My lips tucked into my mouth. He spoke like he was open to being around though. Hopefully, Friday would give more clarity.

A thump in my stomach caused me to gasp and break out of my thoughts. "Shit!" My hands shot to my belly. Over the past few days, I thought I had felt movement in my stomach, but I wasn't completely sure, and this time, I was sure it was movement.

Another movement caused my face to split into a grin. It was obvious both of my kids were up right now. Feeling them right now was unbelievable.

"My troopers," I mumbled, rubbing my stomach.

At my next appointment, I was due to find out the sex of my kids and I couldn't have been more excited.

———

"Look at this belly!" my sister gushed, and her hands went right to my stomach.

"Please don't do that." I slapped her hands away. "What are you doing here?" I closed my door behind her.

I was in the middle of getting ready for Silas' car service to come get me. I tried letting him know earlier that I could drive, but he insisted I got picked up. Since I wasn't trying to argue, I let it go and agreed.

"Can't I come and see my big sister?" Charley bounced over to my couch and sat down.

"Well, I'm about to leave so this has to be a quick visit." I headed back for my bedroom.

"That's why I had to come over. You're never around! Plus, it's going on eight, where you going?"

"You know I started my new job and these babies always have me tired. When I'm not working, all I want to do is sleep."

Charley plopped down on my bed. "Well, I guess that makes sense." Her eyes dropped to my stomach.

"How are my nieces treating you?"

I snorted. "Nieces? How you know they're not boys?"

She balled her face up. "Nah, it's girls. I can feel it."

"Either way, things are fine. I'm just always tired, hungry, and recently horny," I grumbled the last part while putting a few things in my overnight bag.

"Wait are you packing a spinnanight bag? Sis, you got some dick lined up?"

Rolling my eyes, I turned and glared at her. "First off, I'm pregnant so I can't just sleep with anyone. Second no, Silas wants to discuss the babies, so I'm going to his house for the night."

"Even better, sleep with your baby daddy!"

"Charley," I rubbed my temples, "that's not why I'm going over there."

She waved me off. "So what. He's there and the reason you're pregnant anyways. Utilize him." Her shoulders raised.

I chewed on the corner of my bottom lip. The idea had passed through my mind a few times. I had only had sex once, but it was memorable and it was only so much masturbation a person could do after experiencing it.

"Anyways, what's up? The car should be here any minute so talk fast."

"The car?" Her head went back and her hand went to her chest. "Look at rich baby daddy having *a car* come and get you."

I snickered and zipped my bag up. "Shut up."

She grinned. "I didn't want anything. One of my guy friends just moved in one the apartments in the back and I was leaving and decided to stop by."

"Guy friends, huh?" I smirked.

"Yes, friend! Don't give me that look." She rolled her eyes.

"Yeah, okay. Let's go back to the living room."

We headed out my bedroom. "Are you going to bring Silas to Mommy and Daddy's this weekend?" Charley questioned.

My face balled in confusion. "Why would I do that?"

"Well since Myles is coming home and they're cooking out, I thought you would want him to meet the family. You know they both been itching for him to be brought over anyways."

My brows shot up. "Shit! The barbeque," I groaned and rubbed my temples again. I had forgotten that my parents were planning a welcome home barbeque for my brother. He hadn't been home since his winter break and was finally able to come home for the summer.

"Uh, yeah. Did you forget?"

I nodded. "I'll be there." I pressed my lips together. "I don't know about Silas though."

Tonight was up in the air and depending how things turned out would determine a lot going forward.

There was a knock on the door, gaining both of our attention.

"That's probably the car." I slid my feet into my Nike slides. "I'll be at Mom and Dad's. Silas isn't promised."

I opened the door.

"Ms. Jenkins?" the guy questioned.

I nodded. "I'm here to take you to Mr. Newton's. Is that your bag?"

"Yes." I handed the bag to him.

Charley gave me an amused smirk as she walked past me.

"Don't say anything." I grabbed my purse off the small table near my door. Once I locked my house up, I turned to my sister.

"I'll see you Sunday. Don't say anything about Silas coming because I don't know, okay?"

"Yeah, yeah." She waved me off and looked behind me. "Got a car to pick you up. Humph."

"Bye, Charley." I laughed and headed to the black truck waiting in front of my townhouse.

———

The moment I stepped inside Silas' condo, my stomach growled from the sweet aroma inside. I didn't have a preference on what we ate as long as food was involved. Whatever was made smelled delicious.

My bag was in the room I would sleeping in tonight and now me and Silas were sitting at his dining room table, eating in silence. He had his chef prepare smothered chicken with white rice and brown gravy, along with sautéed vegetables and a baked potato.

"I could marry your chef if I get to eat this every day." I moaned, stuffing some rice in my mouth.

Silas' mouth ticked in amusement. He picked up his glass and drank the brown liquid. Not much conversation had passed between us since I been here, but we needed to address the elephant in the room.

Wiping my mouth with my napkin, I focused on Silas. My eyes traced his sharp cheeks, groomed short beard, and wide nose. His eyes reminded me of the smoothest whiskey with a hint of green and when he stared at me too long it felt like I was becoming intoxicated.

He was dressed down in a simple short sleeve button-up and black shorts.

"We should talk about what to expect between us going forward."

"I agree." He finished his drink then sat his glass down. "I've already talked to my accountant and lawyer and had accounts, as well as trust funds, set up for the kids." Silas stood up and walked over to a table that was on the wall behind him. "This is yours. The account set up with that card has more than enough for you to be comfortable and take care of the kids. In the folder, you'll see the accounts I have set up for them. As for the living situations, I own this building and the condo under this one has been vacant since I moved in. I'm having it cleaned so that you and the kids could move in. It's a tad bit smaller than mine, but still three bedrooms and—"

"Stop, stop!" I held my hand up. My head was spinning from the information being thrown at me. I opened the folder up and my eyes nearly popped out my head at the numbers and decimals on the papers. I flipped through them; it was information on three accounts. "Silas." I shifted my eyes up at him.

I knew in his world, money was thrown around and it was the solution for everything, but he was making a lot of decisions without keying me in. I also noticed he referred to our kids as 'the kids' and never our kids.

I ran the back of my hand over my forehead. "First, I don't need your money, Silas. I work and make good money, enough to support our kids. It's not millions like you, but it'll ensure we're comfortable."

He gave me a blank look. "Well, I assumed you would quit your job."

I frowned. "Quit my job? Why would you assume that?"

"You're about to be a mother of two kids. Don't you want to be home with them?" He raised one of his bushy brows and dragged his tongue across his lips.

I shook my head and closed the folder. "No. Do you know how hard I worked to get where I am? All the school I went through? Why would you think I would just quit all that?"

"You'll be taken care of. Is money the reason you feel like that?"

"I don't care about the money! I love what I do, and I worked my ass off to make it happen. I'm not quitting my job and I don't need to be taken care of."

Silas' jaw clenched and his top lip ticked. "And second, what is this about me moving? I have a spare bedroom at my house. The place is big enough for me and the babies."

"No." He shut down. "If you want to work then so be it. The account is yours and the money in it is free for you to use as you please. But the housing is one thing I won't budge on."

"Excuse me?" I pushed away from the table and crossed my arms over my chest.

Silas owned the whole building so the condo under his was vacant, which must've been nice, but I didn't need to move in it.

"You and the kids should be near me. The condo here is a nice size and if you don't want the condo, we'll find a house for you, but being here in New Haven is going to happen. I will not have my kids raised in a city away from me."

Pulling both my lips into my mouth and squinting my eyes, I silently studied him. I pushed a heavy breath through my nose and tilted my head slightly.

"I work in Butter Ridge Falls. How would that be easier for me?"

"Which is why I said you shouldn't work. All you would have to worry about is being home with the kids."

"Our kids," I interjected. "Stop referring to them as the kids. They are *our kids*." I pointed between the two of us.

"I'm aware of that."

Shaking my head, I mentally counted to ten before speaking again. "Silas, look it's obvious you like being in control. It's not a shocker; being who you are, you're used to being in charge, but that doesn't work for me. I'm not one of your employees or kids. I'm a grown woman capable of making choices for me and my children. I *am not* quitting my job nor do I plan on moving out my townhouse. It's enough for me and the babies. The money and everything is nice, and I appreciate you securing our children's future, but they're your responsibility, not me.

My intentions tonight was to discuss co-parenting and how we would handle it. Not you trying to dictate how I live my life and where I live."

Silas cracked his knuckles and rolled his neck between his shoulders.

"I hear you making all these demands but we need to talk about how you feel about the kids and if you plan on being active in their lives."

I wasn't gonna entertain what he was spitting at me at the moment. I had no plans of quitting my job or moving, so there was no reason to keep going back and forth.

"Kids weren't in my future. I personally didn't want to be a father, especially anytime soon. I'm not looking to be tied down." His words made my stomach twist with dread and a lump form in the back of my throat. He cleared his throat. "However, I am a man, and men take care of their responsibilities. I will take care of the, sorry, *our kids*, but I can't promise I'll be good at it."

"We're both gonna be new parents so it won't be perfect, but I'm sure we'll be fine."

He tapped his fingers on the table. "What expectations do you expect from me? Do you expect us to be together?" His orbs pierced into me.

"I don't expect anything but for you to be a father to our children." Movement in my stomach caused my mouth to snapped and eyes to bulge. "Oh," I gasped.

"What?" Concern suddenly filled his face.

"C'mere." I waved him over and rubbed on my stomach.

Silas hurried and pushed out his seat then moved over to me. I grabbed his hand and placed it where our kids were currently going crazy.

"The hell!"

I grinned. "They've been active the past few days," I let him know, moving his hand.

I watched his face to see how he would react. His eyes surprised me by how they lit up. "Damn, does it hurt?" His face balled up.

I shook my head. "No. Just a little weird."

His irises lifted, and he stared at me. They seemed softer than they just were. The moment our eyes connected, my heart stumbled then found its rhythm again. He firmly pressed on where the most movement was making my stomach contract and a rush of heat flooded through my body. Slowly, he licked his lips. The movement of his tongue caused my honey pot to pulsate and tingle.

The tension in the room grew. The air felt as if someone had turned the heat to full blast. My nose slightly flared and my breathing slowed.

I clenched my thighs together.

I don't know how the mood in the room shifted, but I wasn't complaining. The hunger in Silas' eyes increased the wetness forming between my thighs.

Chapter Ten

Silas

My eyes dropped to Indigo's lips. Her tongue dipped between the seams of them, orbs gazed over with need.

My hand was still planted on her stomach, and the kids were still moving around. I lowered my hand until it was on the bottom of her rounded stomach and my finger brushed over her waist. Her nose expanded, and she pushed a heavy breath out while parting her mouth.

I wasn't sure if it was initial but her thighs spread slightly, giving my hand more access to move lower. When she didn't protest, I brushed my fingers over her lower lips through her leggings. Her thighs twitched and her breathing hitched. My eyes stayed locked on hers as I rubbed up and down her sex. Her leggings were damp from her juices.

Biting the corner of my bottom lip, my eyes narrowed, and I used my thumb to press down before circling it.

A small moan fell from her lips. Her eyes fluttered and her hands went to her chair.

Indigo rolled her hips into my touch with her center growing wetter.

Blood rushed to my dick while her cheeks flushed and eyes dilated.

The moment she licked her lips again, I knew I had to taste them.

Dipping my head, I captured her mouth with mine. My hand moved up and slipped into her leggings. Her legs widened more.

I traced the fullness of her lips with the tip of my tongue. I swallowed the moan that fell from her mouth and my tongue made its way inside. I rubbed her button and slid my finger over her soaked slit. She whimpered and gripped my wrist. Her nails dug into my skin.

My dick grew in the shorts I had on.

Our tongues wrestled before I sucked on hers slowly.

My restraint grew thin.

Pulling up, I continued to attack her pussy with my fingers until her body was trembling.

Her breathing picked up and her lashes lowered.

My hand left from inside her leggings and came to my mouth. Hungrily, I sucked her juices, causing the fire inside me to grow hotter.

I grabbed Indigo's hand, urging her to lift. She stared at me with soft eyes and slowly raised from the table.

Since the couch was closer, I led us to the living room and took a seat, removing myself out my shorts. Grabbing the sides of her leggings, she didn't fight me when I pushed them down. Her bald mound came into display. Her bud peeked from between her swollen, soaked lips.

Flickering my eyes up for a second, I reached out and pulled her into me. Hesitancy flashed on her face.

"I got you," I assured her. Gnawing on her bottom lip, she slowly bobbed her head and reached behind her, grabbing my length.

My hands went to her hips as she lowered herself down on me. Her face twisted and mouth parted.

"Silas," she whimpered.

"You can take it. A little more to go," I encouraged.

Her hands went to my shoulders. "Help me," she moaned.

Swiping my tongue across my bottom lip, I started guiding her moments. Her walls were snug around my shaft. It felt like my dick was being drowned by a waterfall.

Moans fell from her mouth as I helped her bounce up and down on my pole until she found her rhythm. Her hips rolled and eyes closed while she tossed her head back.

Her neck was begging for me to taste. My hands went to her locs as I leaned in and sucked on her neck, roughly. My tongue ran down her pulse point, and I sucked her skin into my mouth.

Wanting more of her, I grabbed the hem of her shirt and pulled it up.

Not bothering to remove her sports bra, I pulled her breast out and covered it with my mouth. She clung to my shoulders again.

My tongue swiped across her swollen nipples.

"God!" she cried. Her movement picked up and her pussy gripped tighter.

The night we slept together, I knew for sure I had wrapped up, but it was obvious she was the one percent that it failed. Feeling how snug and warm she felt around me with nothing between us had me ready to shoot off.

Kissing and sucking my way up until I got to her lips, I possessed them again. She leaned closer and her stomach rubbed against mine.

My hands went back to her hips, and I thrusted upwards as I took over her movements.

"Just like that," I growled. My teeth sank to my bottom lip.

I glanced down, watching my dick disappear in and out of her.

Her body jerked and trembled on top of me. Soon as the flood between her legs grew wetter, I was releasing inside her. My fingers sank into her sides.

Indigo bit into my bottom lip as she rode her orgasm and her body twitched above me.

"Fuck. I needed that." I panted the moment she pulled away.

Her lips were swollen, eyes low, and breathing heavy. I loved how dismantled she currently looked.

She gave me a shaky smile before leaning in and resting her forehead on my shoulder. "You feel a'right?" I questioned.

I wasn't sure the protocol with sex when it came to pregnant women, and I didn't even stop to think.

Lazily, she nodded.

My hand ran up her naked skin, cuffing her stomach.

"They're moving again," she whispered, her voice slightly raspy.

A couple seconds passed through us before Indigo lifted and climbed off me. Her cheeks were still flushed, and her forehead was covered with beads of sweat.

"I'm going to go shower," she let me know, barely meeting my eye.

Bending down, she grabbed her leggings and headed out my living room without waiting for me to say anything. Truthfully, I didn't expect to have sex with her tonight. It hadn't crossed my mind, but I wasn't complaining. I didn't want to give Indigo the wrong idea with us. Although I learned she was having my kids, I still wasn't tryna be locked down. Sex with her wasn't bad though, and I wouldn't mind repeating it.

My eyes dropped to my flaccid dick that sat on my thigh. Seeing it slick with Indigo's juices almost made me rock back up.

Turning my head, I glanced in the direction of the bedrooms. I had half a mind to join her in the shower but decided against it. The release she gave me was more than needed and would hold me over for now.

———

I was in the middle of eating my breakfast while going over some investments and bets I'd taken this week.

Indigo was still sleep, and from what I assumed, she'd fallen right to sleep after her shower last night. I was typically an early riser and enjoyed having this moment to myself.

A knock on the door caused me to pause in the middle of drinking my orange juice. My brows crinkled, wondering who would come here uninvited. Not too many people had the code to gain access to my place.

Seeing whoever wasn't going to leave, I went to my camera app and pulled up my front door. The moment I saw my mom standing outside my door, my blood ran cold and I groaned.

I debated if I wanted to answer or act like I wasn't home.

The knocking grew louder. Knowing my mother, she knew I was here and wouldn't go away until I answered.

Sighing, I had to bite the bullet.

Pushing away from my table, I made my way to door, turned the alarm off, unlocked it, and pulled it open.

"It's not polite to keep your mother waiting, Silas!" she nagged and barged past me.

My hand went to the back of my neck, and I gripped it tightly.

"It's nine in the morning, Mother, some people sleep at this time."

She waved me off and looked around. "I knew you were up." When she spun around, she pushed her sunglasses up, narrowed her eyes, and studied me.

"You're avoiding me again."

"I'm not avoiding you. I do have a company to run." My arms crossed.

She rolled her eyes. "You're so busy you can't take two seconds to respond back to your mother. It could have been an emergency." I stared at her blankly.

I wasn't about to get wrapped into this.

"What can I do for you, Mom?"

Her lips pressed together. "Spencer said she reached out to you, but you blew her off."

"I told you I wasn't interested in you setting me up."

Her eyes grew tighter. "Spencer is a nice, respectable girl, Silas! She comes from a great family. She has great genes and would make a wonderful wife."

"I'm not looking for a wife."

"You should be. You're not getting any younger, son." Her eyes went around the living room and suddenly froze.

I turned in the direction she was looking and bit back a groan as Indigo stood there. She had on a small t-shirt that barely covered her stomach and shorts. "Uh, sorry, I smelt food." Her eyes bounced between me and my mom. "Am I interrupting?"

My mom stuck her nose up and mouth twisted as if she'd sucked a lemon. "Silas, who is this woman? And what is wrong with her stomach?"

This wasn't going to end well. I could already see the car crash happening so I decided to deploy the air bags early.

Making my way to Indigo, I placed my hand on the small of her back. "Indigo this is Pamela, my mom. Mom, this is Indigo." I cleared my throat. "The mother of your grandchildren."

For the first time in my life, I saw my mother speechless. The color drained from her face and her body grew more rigid.

"Excuse me!" she shrieked. "She's what?"

Indigo stepped forward. "It's nice to meet you, Pam." She held her hand out.

"It's Pamela." Instead of taking it like a normal human, my mom glanced down as if she had shit on it. "Actually, Mrs. Newton. Silas, this is not funny. Who is this woman and why is she here?"

"I just told you who she is. Indigo is having my kids."

"No. That's not possible." She looked Indigo up and down, not bothering to hide her disgust. "Sweetheart, if it's money you want then you're barking up the wrong tree."

Indigo's hand dropped, and she stepped back. "I don't need your son's money." Her voice was now tight.

My mom's eyes cut to me. "Silas, you shouldn't believe any woman who claims to have your kids without a test."

I stepped forward so I was back at Indigo's side. "I did get a test. Indigo is having twins and they're mine. I'm having those kids you been wanting for me."

My mom looked like she was seconds away from passing out. "This is unacceptable! Silas do you understand who you are? Do you know what it will look like having a baby by some random hussy!"

"Hussy!" Indigo's head cocked back.

"Yes, hussy! I don't know how you trapped my son, but I won't stand for it. Do you think Spencer will want you knowing you got this woman pregnant?" My mom waved her arm in front of Indigo.

"Silas, I'm being respectful because this is your mother, but I'm two seconds away from losing that respect. Lady, get your hand out my face." Her eyes cut into tight slits.

Hearing the bite in her voice shocked me.

"You're going to let her talk to your mother like that?" Mom grabbed her chest.

I needed to shut this down.

Stepping between them, I looked between them. "Mom, Indigo is having my children. It's been confirmed. You have to accept that."

Mom scuffed. "The hell I do! Just wait until your father hears about this!" She didn't wait for anyone to reply.

I watched as my mom spun around on her heels and stormed for my front door.

My hands went to my temples, and I attempted to rub out the headache forming.

"There's enough food for you in the kitchen," I finally told Indigo and headed back for the table.

When I noticed she didn't move, I stared at her. Her arms were crossed and mouth balled up. "We're not going to talk about that?"

"About what?"

"About what? How about how disrespectful your mother just was!" She tossed her hands up.

"I handled it."

"You really didn't! You let her disrespect me and our kids."

"My mom is just opinionated. Don't take anything she says to heart." I took a seat.

Growing up, I mastered learning how to zone my mom out and stop allowing her to get to me. She was stubborn and bullheaded. It was better to let her rant then move on.

"Are you serious?"

Sighing, I rubbed my eyes. "Look, Ima handle my mom. Right now the easiest thing to do was not encourage it. I'll go talk to her and handle it."

Indigo glared at me with a frown etched on her pretty face. "I had the chef make you a plate before he left. It's over there in the kitchen. Sit down and I'll grab it. Don't worry about my mom."

I walked over to the plate that was wrapped on the counter, grateful it was still warm. When I turned around, Indigo was pouring orange juice into her glass. Placing the plate in front of her, I went and returned to my seat across the table.

Silently, we ate for a moment with the air still slightly tensed. Leave it to my mom to come in and kill the mood.

"We should talk." Indigo cut the silence after a few seconds.

Lifting my eyes and giving her my attention, I waited for her to continue. "What did last night mean?" She shoved a scoop of eggs in her mouth.

I raised a brow. "We had sex."

Her eyes rolled upwards. "I know that." Her words drawled. "But what does that mean? We're having kids together, so I believe we need to create boundaries and lay everything on the table. We don't know one another, and I would like to change that since for the rest of our lives we're tied to one another."

Indigo had her locs in a ponytail resting on her neck. Her face glowed and looked freshly washed. While studying her, I noticed how delicately carved her facial bones were and how full her lips were.

Her brows rose inquiringly as she waited for me to respond.

"I don't want to be tied down. My whole life I dealt with my parents, mainly my mother, making choices for me. Having the freedom to move around as I please and not answer to anyone is a plea-sure to me." Her orbs filled with a curious, deep longing. "However, I do agree we should get to know each other more. As for sex, I'm down to give it to you whenever we both want it." A sly grin slid onto my face.

She drew her lips in thoughtfully and her mouth thinned. "So you want to be fuck buddies?" Her head cocked to the side.

My shoulders lifted. "If that's what you want to call it. I call it co-parenting with benefits."

Indigo picked up her orange juice, and I watched as she watched me over her glass. "No." The moment she removed the glass from her lips, she licked the remaining juice away and pouted her lips out.

"No." Here tone was bland. "We can co-parent, that I agree on. If you don't want anything serious I'm fine with that, but I won't lower myself to being a booty call." Her nose scrunched up.

A crooked grin appeared on my face. "You make it sound so dirty. We're two adults. Sex isn't wrong."

"I'm not saying it is. Sex is new to me, but that doesn't mean I'm going to just accept anything."

Her words were displeasing to me, but I wasn't going to fight it. If she wanted to cut sex out between us then so be it. It would complicate things less anyways.

"Okay. I get it. I'm not going to force you into anything." My hands went up.

Indigo's shoulders relaxed and fell forward. "Good. So getting to know each other more is the most important thing. I would like us to be friends at least by the time the kids come." She pressed her lips together and eyes squinted for a second. "Which reminds me. My parents are having a barbeque tomorrow for my brother who's coming home from college. I would like for you to come."

My eyebrows drew together then raised. "You would?"

With a slight dip of her head, her face split into a slight grin. "You getting to meet my parents and my family is important to me. It may not be what you're used to, but I can guarantee you good food."

My hand flexed, and I thought over what she said. As far as I knew, I had a clear day tomorrow. I tried to keep Sundays free. From the background check I did, I knew almost everything on the surface when it came to Indigo, but it would probably help if I went a bit deeper. Learning the people who would be around my kids would be important.

"Okay."

"Okay?"

"Yes, okay. Send me the time and location and I'll be there."

Her smile grew. "Good."

Her eyes dropped back to her plate.

Like a creep, I kept my eyes planted on her and watched as she ate. It seemed everything about Indigo was feminine. She wasn't even trying to be but it seemed she moved with grace as she ate.

Indigo must have felt my eyes still on her because she glanced up and curiosity bounced around in her orbs. When I didn't speak, she gave me a shy grin and went back to eating.

This was the first time I had been in a situation like this with a female, but from being around Indigo the few times I had, I believed it would be an easy time.

Chapter Eleven

Indigo

"Oh damn; when I was told you were pregnant, I didn't know you were this pregnant!" My baby brother's eyes bulged the moment they landed on my stomach.

I snickered and gave him a small nudge. "Oh hush! C'mere!" I pulled him as close as I could and hugged him tightly. "I missed you, big head." I kissed the top of his head before releasing him. .

"I missed you too. I'm sorry again about missing your graduation." I waved him off.

"Don't worry about it. I'm just happy to see you now. You look like you've been in the gym." I poked his arms.

He flexed with a smirk on his face. "Well, you know."

Rolling my eyes, I snickered again.

"Don't pump his head up any more than it already is." Charley approached us.

"And the ugly sister arrives."

"I'll show you ugly." She pulled him into a tight hug before giving him a nuggie.

"Watch the waves."

I shook my head at the two. They were always fussing with one another. I knew it wouldn't take long to start.

"Don't y'all start!" my dad's voice sounded. "Y'all ain't been here ten minutes and already acting like y'all weren't raised right."

"That's your daughter. She needs to be tamed!" His eyes cut to our sister, who lifted her middle finger.

I shook my head and walked over to my dad. "Hi, Daddy!" I hugged him.

"Indi, baby girl. How these two treatin' you?" He eyed my stomach.

I rubbed it slowly and shrugged. "Fine, draining all my energy, but it's nothing I can't handle."

"When do you find out the sex?"

"Next week!" I beamed. At first, I was gonna wait until I delivered, but I was too excited to learn what I was having and I wouldn't be able to hold out.

My dad looked around. "And where is the father?"

"He's coming, don't worry." Playfully, I rolled my eyes.

"I can't wait to meet rich baby daddy!"

My eyes cut to my sister. "Can you not call him that when he gets here?"

"I told you she needs to be tamed." My brother walked up. "He better come correct that's all I know." He narrowed his eyes at me.

"Boy!" I waved Myles off. He was the youngest but was always so protective of both me and Charley.

"Okay, let me get back out to the grill. Myles, come help me. Everyone should be arriving room. Girls, go see if your mom needs help in the kitchen."

I groaned. "I'm pregnant. Can't I just sit and wait to eat?"

"No! Get in here," my mom called out, making both my siblings laugh.

Knowing there was no getting out of it, I headed for the kitchen. Normally, I didn't mind cooking with my mom, but with all the food and having to wait to eat was torture.

"I got the stuff, Auntie." Audrey came blaring through the kitchen a few moments later.

"Good, set them on the table and wash your hands."

Times like this reminded me when I was younger. We always did stuff like this, Audrey included. I was excited we were all getting together. I was even more excited my baby brother was home. We were the furthest away in age, but truthfully, we were just as close as me and Charley.

———

"Okay, Mom, enough pictures," I whined, ready to sit back down. The barbeque was going well, but she didn't know how to do anything small. What was supposed to be a small gathering of close family and friends turned out to be more than that.

My mom couldn't let the day go by without taking a million pictures of me and my siblings; not to mention, too many people were trying to touch my stomach and I was getting annoyed. I was ready to call it a day, but I was trying to be a team player.

I had managed to dodge the questions about Silas not being here, thankfully. He told me he was coming and that's all I knew.

"Okay, honey, that's enough." My dad came and wrapped his arm around my mom's shoulders and kissed her temple. Silently, I thanked him and made my way over to where I was previously sitting, taking a detour to grab another plate.

Just as I was about to sit down, my phone dinged on the table. When I glanced down, I saw it was Silas texting me. The day was halfway over, and I started to believe he wouldn't make it. Picking my phone up, I saw he was letting me know he had made it.

For some reason, knowing he was here, made my nerves rattle and stomach flip.

Setting my phone down, I headed towards the house and made my way around it instead of going inside. The music playing in the back-yard could be heard lowly towards the front of the house.

"Hey!" I approached Silas, who was waiting on the front porch.

Spinning around, he gave me a once-over before his mouth lifted into a smile. "Hi." The black and white Calvin Klein short sleeve shirt he had on was nice on his muscular chest, causing me to admire him for a second.

"Everyone's in the back." I nodded my head in the direction I'd come from. I had already begged my family to act like they had sense and not treat Silas like some museum when he got here. I didn't want anyone hounding him or making it weird just because he came from money. His hands slid in his white shorts and he followed behind me.

"You look nice." Glancing over my shoulder, I noticed his eyes on my ass. The sundress I had on fit perfectly with my growing size.

"Thanks." He snatched his eyes up and slyly grinned.

Thankfully, when we got to the back, everyone was lost in their own worlds not noticing I had dipped off. I hoped to be able to just introduce him to my parents then the two of us can duck off to where I was sitting.

Silas letting me know he wasn't looking for anything serious made it easier to draw lines with us. We could parent platonically and focus on our kids without all the extra stuff.

I eyed the yard, and when I found my parents, I grabbed Silas' hand and pulled him in that direction. "My parents have been looking forward to meeting you. My mom is a bit extra, I'm letting yo know now. My dad is pretty chilled."

He snorted. "I deal with million dollar deals every day and uptight CEOs. I'm sure I can handle your parents."

Not bothering to say anything else, I approached my parents, who were having a conversation, and stood in front of them.

"Mom, Dad," I interrupted.

Their conversation paused and their attention turned to me.

The moment they noticed Silas, my mom's eyes lit up and my dad's face went blank.

"This is Silas. Silas, my parents. Tiara and Noah."

Silas stepped forward. "It's nice to meet both of you." My dad was the first to grab his hand. He stared at Silas with a fixed expression.

"Nice to meet you." My dad's voice a pitch deeper than Silas', but Silas didn't falter, he kept my dad's eye contact.

"Okay, that's enough." My mom hit my dad's shoulder.

"It's nice to meet you, honey." Finally, the guys released hands and Silas turned to my mom this time with a smile on his face.

"Considering the circumstances, I hoped we would meet sooner."

"Daddy," I warned.

"The situation caught us both off guard. I think the timing is perfect."

My eyes widened and snapped to Silas.

My mom shook her head. "Okay, Indi, go take Silas to get a plate and we'll meet you guys where you're sitting."

Doing as my mom said, I grabbed Silas and led him away. I could already see my dad's and Silas' personalities clashing and hoped today didn't end on bad note.

"Oh sister!" Charley bounced over to us just as we approached the food. Audrey was at her side.

Charley was grinning ear to ear as she gazed at Silas. "Who is this?"

Rolling my eyes, I quickly did the introductions.

"You two favor," Silas noted, looking between me and my sister.

"Eh, you think?" I glanced at Charley. I always felt like my younger siblings favored my mom more and I took more after my dad.

"I do." Silas stated.

"I think that's the first time we've heard that." Charley laughed.

"That's because you two are like night and day. No one who knows y'all would think anything is similar," Audrey threw in.

I stood to the side as Silas made his plate. "You did good, sis," Charley leaned over and told me in a hushed voice.

"No foreal. He's fine online, but finer in person." Out the corner of my eyes, I watched Silas.

"Can you two please stop?" Heat flushed my cheeks.

"We're just saying. Look at how big his shoes are." Audrey smirked.

"Can probably do some damage." Charley agreed.

Ignoring the two of them while they went on, I led Silas to the coolers so I could grab us something to drink then to the table. My eyes lit up, remembering I had made a plate before he arrived.

While we sat and ate, a few family members came over to meet him. I was grateful that they didn't overdo it.

My cousin and sister took a seat across from us and spent the next couple minutes questioning Silas.

"You could have come and told me your baby daddy was here," my brother's voice sounded behind us.

I finished the rib I was eating and glanced behind me.

"You were busy." I waved him off.

When he approached us, he gave Silas the same look as our dad. "Silas, my brother, Myles. Myles, Silas." I grabbed another rib. My kids were happy about the food I had consumed. I knew after I finished this plate, I would useless for the rest of the day.

"So you're the guy who knocked my sister up?"

"Myles!"

"Myles!" My mom walked up behind him and slapped the back of his head.

"Ow!" He flinched.

"Be nice."

Her and my dad took a seat at the table.

"I'm glad you were able to come and join us today," my mom started.

"Thank you for inviting me."

A smile formed on my mom's face. "Of course. Meeting the man who's fathered our first grandkids is important. You're family now."

"That's to be determined."

"Preach, Dad." My brother took a seat. His eyes cut to my brother for a moment before coming back to Silas.

"I want to know how my daughter and her kids fit into your world," my dad started.

I chewed on the inside of my jaw. His was voice stern.

Silas grabbed a napkin and wiped his mouth before giving my dad his attention. "I don't understand what you mean. My kids and their mother will be taken care of."

"You mean financially?"

"Yes."

"And what about physically and emotionally? It's a lot more to being a parent than throwing money at something."

"I never said I was planning on throwing money at anyone. Me and Indigo have come up with a plan to co-parent."

"Co-parent as in you two won't be together? You plan on my child being a single mother?"

"I wouldn't call it being a single mother, but yes co-parent. I don't want a relationship right now."

"And I'm too focused on my career and now being a new mom to date, Daddy."

"However, I do plan on forming a friendship with Indigo. We're going to have to be around each other a lot, and I would like us to be close."

"And how does your family feel about this? Do they accept my daughter?"

Silas was quiet and my eyes dropped. My run-in yesterday with his mom flashed through my mind. It ground my gears how she looked down at me, but I was trusting Silas would set her straight.

"My mom wasn't accepting when she first found out, but she was caught off guard. She's been wanting grandkids for a while, and I have no doubt she'll be happy."

"But will she be happy with my daughter?" This time, my mom asked the question.

Silas turned to look at me. I gave him a small grin. "I believe once she gets to know Indigo, she will."

"And what about you? Do you feel like my sister isn't good enough to be with?"

I glared in my brother's direction. "Myles, you're doing too much."

"I'm not doing enough." He poked his chest out. "Just because he's made of money, does he feel like you're not good enough to be more than his baby mama?"

Silas' face was still but not upset. He stared at my brother with a calm expression. "I never said your sister wasn't good enough nor have I referred to her as my baby mama, as you say. I just do not want to be tied down at the moment, whether I was having kids or not. I think your sister is a lovely person, she's intelligent, and would make a great addition to my family."

My heart swelled and a fire lit inside it. The smile on my face couldn't be hidden. "That she is. My Indi is a catch, and any man would be lucky to have her," my mom bragged.

"Even you, Money Bags."

"Charley!" She snickered and tossed her hands up.

"Enough." My dad's face was still blank. His eyes hadn't left Silas. "I respect your choice, and if my daughter and you have come to an agreement, we *all* will respect that as well. As long as you pull your weight as the twins' father and my daughter is happy, then I'm happy," he finally said and it made me relax more.

"I'll do whatever I can to make sure all three are happy and taken care of." They seemed to have some silent conversation.

Thankfully, once my dad spoke everyone lightened up, and the questions with Silas got lighter. I wasn't sure how he would be with my family, but he seemed to be settling in fine with them. Of course, my sister and Audrey dragged him off, and I could only imagine what was said. When I looked, he seemed to be amused by whatever the conversation was.

Myles kept mugging him, but he kept his opinion to himself. I was joyous to see him and my dad sharing a beer towards the end of the night.

"He doesn't seem too bad." My mom walked over and took a seat next to me.

The yard had started to clear out, and I knew it wouldn't be long before she started cleaning up.

"He's not. A little controlling, but I think he's a good guy."

My mom's attention went to my dad and child's father. "Just be careful, Indigo. I can see on your face you're fond of him. Don't start getting invested and be the only one."

I turned my head to stare at the side of her face. "Trust me, I won't. I'm good."

It wasn't long before my dad and Silas were making their way to us. My body now felt achy and exhausted.

"I think it's time for you to go home and get in the bed," my mom commented. I smiled at her with exhausted eyes and nodded.

"I agree."

"Are you up to drive?" I waved her off.

"I'll be fine. A little sleepiness isn't gonna kill me."

"Still, you look like you could barely keep your eyes open."

Silas stared at me with concern. "If you're too tired…"

"I'm not."

He ignored me. "Then, I can follow you home."

"I would feel better about that." Mom let him know.

Shaking my head, I pushed out a heavy breath. "Fine."

After saying my goodbyes, I grabbed my to-go dishes and headed for my car.

"You don't have to follow me," I told Silas.

"But I am."

Not bothering to fight him, I went and got in my car. Although I knew I could make the fifteen-minute drive and be fine, I was impressed that Silas offered to make sure I got there safely.

Chapter Twelve

Silas

The moment I stepped inside my parents' house, I felt my energy drop. My parents' house always felt too big for my comfort. Growing up as an only kid, I never understood why my parents needed such a large home. They proclaimed they loved the space, but I knew it was because they wanted to brag about it.

I wasn't sure how the conversation I was about to have would go, but I had to set things straight. Hopefully, by the time I left, my parents would be more accepting to the fact that Indigo was pregnant.

My mom and dad were in the family room, both on their laptops.

"Hey y'all," I spoke up, gaining their attention.

My mom turned her mouth up. "I wish you wouldn't use that word, Silas."

Shaking my head, I approached her and kissed her cheek. "It's good seeing you too, Mom. Dad." I nodded to my dad and took a seat in the chair next to the couch they were sitting on.

"I need to talk to y'all."

My mom stared at me with an etched expression on her face while my dad's was blank. "I'm sure Mom has already told you Dad, but in a few months, you're going to be a grandfather of twins."

My eyes snapped to my mom when her laptop slammed shut. Her lips pinched together tightly.

"Silas, I wasn't going to entertain this then and I won't now," she stated.

Drawing my brows together, I tightened my stare on her. "Entertain what, exactly? The fact that I'm about to have kids? Isn't this what you wanted?"

"I did not tell you to go out and get some random woman pregnant! We don't know that girl, nor do we know anything about her family or what she wants. How do you know she isn't after your money? Is her family even decent? You can't just go around procreating with just anyone, Silas."

"You're mother's right, Silas. You can't just come in here and tell us you're having a baby with some woman we know nothing about. We have a certain image to uphold, you know."

Dragging my tongue over the top of my teeth, I flexed my hands and rolled my shoulders. My eyes bounced between the two of them.

I know how I handled things at first when it came to Indigo wasn't ideal, but I wasn't going to allow my parents to paint her out to be a person she wasn't.

"Indigo doesn't have any ulterior motives when it comes to me. Her getting pregnant was an accident. Neither of us planned it, but we're handling it together."

"By handling do you mean she's getting rid of it?" I stared at my mom, trying to see if she was serious. By the look on her face, she was.

"No. Why would you think that?"

"You said she was handling it. If you decide to have kids it needs to be with someone of our stature, Silas. Gosh, have we taught you nothing." My mom scoffed and turned her nose up.

"This isn't the 1800s. Just because Indigo isn't as rich as us doesn't mean she's below us nor do I have to feel ashamed that she's having my kids because you two want to judge her by her bank account."

My parents shared a look then turned their attention back to me with an unenthusiastic expression.

"Silas, we didn't make sure you have the life you have to just go out and share that wealth with just anyone. If you're going to be with someone then it should be with someone who will add to your life."

My mouth turned. "I never mentioned us being together."

"So not only are you having a child by some nameless hussy, but you don't even plan on being with her. This just keeps getting better and better." My mom brushed some hair out her face and folded her hands in her lap.

My temples throbbed, and I knew it was time to wrap things up here. "I didn't come here for either of your approval. Indigo is due in four months, and whether you two like it or not, the twins are mine and I *will* be in their lives. If you two don't approve then you don't have to be a part of their lives, but I'm not going to let you convince me that Indigo isn't worthy enough to have my kids."

Indigo didn't come from a bad family; they were middle class and her parents had done well for themselves. She was probably the smartest woman I had ever been with too, not that my parents would know this because they didn't even bother to try and learn anything about her.

The doorbell went off, but no one moved, knowing the staff would get it. My dad had went back to whatever he was doing on his laptop, obviously finished with the conversation. While my mom continued to bore a hole into me.

"You know, Silas, your whole life you have gone against what me and your father have wanted for you. Never mind we have your best interest at heart, but you just ignore that and do whatever you want and now look what happened! If you would have just listened to us, then you wouldn't be in this situation that we must clean up!"

Narrowing my eyes, I leaned forward and widened my legs. "What are you talking about handle it? Nothing needs to be handled but—"

Before I could finish my statement, a body stepping into the family room caught my eyes.

"Hi. I'm sorry I'm late."

"Oh, no. Spencer, honey, you're right on time. Come, come. Take a seat!" My mom grinned.

Biting the inside of my jaw, I watched as Spencer went and took a seat next to my mom. "I'm so glad you were able to make it. You remember my son, Silas."

My expression dropped as my jaw tightened. I should have expected something like this from my mom.

"Hello, Silas. It's nice to see you again."

I scanned her over. Spencer was a cute girl. She had the girl next-door thing going on. Soft feminine features, honey-colored skin with large doe eyes, and light brown hair that rested on her shoulders.

"What is this?" I ignored Spencer and glared at my mom.

"Silas, don't be rude. Spencer spoke to you."

"Wassup." I nodded, causing my mom to frown deeper.

"Spencer, please excuse my son's behavior right now. He's going through some things at the moment, but it's getting handled. I'm glad you were able to make it so you two could finally reconnect." The smile was back on mom's face.

"This is ridiculous." I shook my head and stood up.

"Silas, what are you doing?"

"I told you I didn't need to be set up with anyone. I didn't come here for this either." I looked at Spencer. "It's no disrespect towards you, but I'm not interested. Sorry my mom wasted your time."

I was sure steam was blowing out my mom's ears by how angry she looked. Turning on my heels, I started for the exit. Obviously, I wasn't going to get anywhere with this conversation and my mom inviting Spencer here showed she had ulterior motives I wanted no parts of.

———

"I can't believe we're about to learn the sex of our kids. I feel like this pregnancy is flying by," Indigo gushed.

My eyes scanned around the examination room.

"Yeah, this shit's flying by." I tapped my fingers against my knee. Realizing in a short couple of months that I would be a father to two kids had me jittery. After my meet up with my parents failed, I needed something else to focus on.

"I've been buying neutral baby things but it'll be nice to finally be able to set their rooms up." Indigo was set on staying at her house, but I was determined to get her to move in my building. "Have you started shopping for them yet?"

"No, once we find out the sex I'll have Fiona order somethings." The look that passed over Indigo's face had me about to question it when a knock on the door happened.

A few seconds later, Dr. Hill entered the room.

"Today's the big day!" She grinned, looking between us. "Any concerns?" She walked to the sink to go wash her hands.

"Nope. Besides the excitement building up inside me."

"Well let's not keep you waiting."

The first appointment I might not have been as present mentally, but now that I knew the kids were mine, I was focused.

Dr. Hill did her examination of Indigo, and once she was finished, she got everything set up for the sonogram.

"Here goes the gel." Moving my seat closer, I leaned in with my eyes locked on the screen.

After a few clicks of buttons, the heartbeats of the twins filled the room. When I looked at Indigo's face, I couldn't help but smile at how she beamed. Her eyes were wide and bright and a smile filled her whole face.

"Sounds good. Healthy." She hit a few more buttons. "Now let's get to the fun part."

Dr. Hill pointed out different features of the babies, showing us different body parts.

"Baby A is not shy at all." She snickered and glanced at us. My heart thumped erratically for a moment. "Looks like we have identical boys! Congratulations, you two!"

My eyes shot open at the mention of me having boys. I hadn't really considered what I wanted the twins to be. It didn't really seem real until right now. The sex didn't really matter to me but hearing I would be having sons sent a warmness through my body and pride filled my chest.

Indigo grabbed my hand and gave it a squeeze. "Can you believe it! Two boys!" she gushed.

"Shit, twin boys." Amazement passed through me.

"I'll print you both pictures. Then, we'll wrap things up."

I couldn't keep my eyes off the motion. This whole time I had been fighting that I was about to be a dad, but something in this moment shifted for me.

Dr. Hill finished up the appointment, and I stayed to the side while she and Indigo wrapped things up.

"Do you mind if we make a stop before you drop me off?" Indigo questioned once we were in my car.

Pulling out the parking lot of the doctor's, I glanced at her quickly. "My schedule's free." She smiled softly.

"Good, I was hoping you said that."

Out the corner of my eye, I watched her. She was grinning widely and tapping quickly on her phone. "My sister is gonna be so mad I'm not having girls." She giggled.

Hearing how excited she was about the twins made me want to record and send it to my parents. They had so much doubt about Indigo, but I was sure she wasn't a bad choice to have kids with.

———

When Indigo asked to make a stop, I didn't think she meant shopping. There was a baby store, I wasn't aware of, near the mall that we were currently walking through. She seemed to be in her own world, picking out things for the twins while I followed along, making mental notes of everything.

I had no clue what I needed to prepare for two babies coming, but watching Indigo was giving me an idea. If all else failed, I would hire someone to come in and prepare their nursey.

"Oooo, I heard this bottle warmer is good." She picked up the box and examined it before putting it in the cart. So far she had filled it with clothes, bibs, blankets, bottles, and a few other things I didn't catch.

"We need to go over to the cribs. I was on their site a couple days ago and saw two I couldn't choose between so I want to look at both." Indigo didn't even give me a glance. I pushed the cart while she waddled in front of me.

"I think their room will be done in a safari theme. Now that I know the sex, I can start planning more effectually."

Scrunching my nose, I paused when we got to the cribs. "Safari? Why?"

Her shoulders lifted and she glanced over her shoulder at me. "Animals interest me. Maybe it's the nerd in me. Oh, there's one of the cribs."

She waddled over, and I looked at the items in front of us. "Which one do you like more?" She pointed between the two.

I didn't really see the difference in the two, but I went with the one I felt looked better. "That one." I pointed.

"That's the one I was learning towards." She grinned. "Shit, kids are expensive." She groaned, looking at the tags.

Frowning, I glanced down. The store we were in seemed worth the hefty price, but everything Indigo had picked up including the cribs wouldn't even put a dent in the account I set up for her.

She took a picture of the price tag and then turned to me. "Okay, I'm hungry and think I've done enough damage for the day." Her eyes went to the cart that was full to the top.

"Whatever you want." I shrugged.

I wasn't an instore shopping person, typically I liked online, but I didn't mind walking around the store with Indigo. All I had to do was push the cart and help her decide here and there on things she was between. I ended up convincing her just to get both since we were having two babies.

When we got to the register, I watched as the person behind the counter began to scan the items as Indigo set them on the belt. "I want to order two cribs too," she mentioned towards the end.

The guy behind the counter nodded.

My phone vibrated and gained my attention. I saw I had a text from my mom, which I ignored, and then one from Fiona asking me to confirm a meeting I had tomorrow. I also had a text in the darts group chat about our meet up tomorrow evening.

After replying to everyone, I looked up just in time to hear the total price.

Indigo nodded but before she was able to go into her purse to pay, I was using my phone to pay.

"I didn't ask you to bring me to pay for me." She stared at me blankly.

"I wish I would let you pay for things for our kids while I'm standing here." I signed for the purchase.

She studied me intensely before a small grin broke out on her face. "What?" I nodded at her when he held out the receipt.

She shook her head bashfully. "This is the first time I heard you refer to the twins as both of ours."

Bunching my brows together, I thought about what she said and then went over what I just told her. "Well, they are *ours*." I shrugged.

Her smile grew and I grabbed the cart.

We headed out the store to my car. Thankfully, I drove my truck today since I knew Indigo would need the room because of her growing stomach.

While Indigo got inside, I loaded the bags inside. She attempted to help but I shut it down completely.

After loading my truck, I climbed in the truck and glanced over. "You said you were hungry. What do you want to eat?"

Turning to face me, she gave me a shocked expression.

"What?"

Her eyes slightly lowered. "I just...something's different about you today. I don't know what it is, but you're not so demanding today, I guess."

I chuckled and dragged my hand over my mouth. "Yeah, well you better utilize it while you can."

She snickered. "Can we go to that Italian place?" She pointed across the street.

I nodded and started my Range Rover.

———

"Even though I ate this morning, I feel like it's been ages." Indigo practically inhaled the pasta on her plate, causing my eyes to widen. I had never seen someone eat so quickly.

"It's not going anywhere. Slow down before you choke." She giggled and grabbed her lemonade.

Cutting into my lasagna, I shoved a piece into my mouth. She seemed in total bliss as she ate.

"I spoke to my mother," I assured her, causing her to glance up at me. She cut her eyes and sucked some noodles up.

"How did that go?"

"Let's just say it went." I flashed a crooked smile. "It doesn't matter though; my parents don't determine any choices in my life."

"So neither of them are happy about the twins?" She placed her fork down, giving me her full attention. Her lips twisted to the side.

"My parents are old school. They believe money should be with money and all that shit. That's not how I see things or live my life. So if they aren't on board it's no skin off my bones."

Creases formed in her forehead, and she leaned back. "But I would have liked both set of grandparents around."

I chortled. "Trust me, the twins are better off without my parents. They're a bit much, mainly my mother."

I flexed my hand and dropped my eyes to it. I loved my parents, but I wouldn't allow them to run my kids' childhood like they did mine.

"Do you believe in nature vs. nurture?" Indigo asked suddenly.

Confusion filled my face. "What?" I brought my eyes back up to meet hers.

"Like your environment shapes who you are over genetics? It's been a debate in the science and psychology community forever."

Still lost on her point, I lifted my shoulders. "Never really gave it any thought. Why?"

"It's just interesting seeing how you are compared to what I assume your parents are just from meeting your mom. Is that why you're so controlling? Do you believe how you were raised shaped you and not because of who your parents are?" She raised a brow.

Smirking, I stabbed my food with my fork and stuck another piece inside my mouth. "I guess you can say that. Not in the way you're thinking though. My whole life was planned out from the moment I was born. Growing up, my mom was in control of how I dressed, who I hung around, where I went, how I thought. She had this image of the perfect child she wanted to mold me into and once I got older, I started breaking that mold, tired of being controlled. Once I started gaining control of my own life, I knew I never wanted to feel chained down again." I shrugged. "Now I live how I want by my own rules."

Her lashes brushed over her cheeks and here orbs softened. "Is that why you're so against being in a relationship? You feel like you'll be chained down."

My bottom lip tucked in between my teeth, and I sat back in my chair. "You can say that. I don't like the thought of answering to anyone or being tied to one person. It's all I knew growing up so being able to do as I please with who I please is rejuvenating for me."

Slowly, she nodded. I could see her mind working. "I guess that makes sense." Her nose scrunched up. "It sucks that's what your child-hood led you to though."

Again, I shrugged. "It's been working for me. Kids weren't in the plans, but I can handle change." I grew quiet for a moment. "What about you? There's got to be a reason why you waited so long to have sex and you're single."

She snorted. "No, not really." She looked around the restaurant then back to me. "I didn't stay a virgin because I wanted to wait until marriage or even the right one." Her cheeks reddened as our server approached. Her cheeks matched Indigo.

"Everything good?" she asked, blinking rapidly.

"We're good, sweetheart. Can you grab us the bill?" I looked at the plates. "And to-go containers?"

"Can I have more lemonade too?"

"Coming right up." She didn't give Indigo a second glance and hurried off.

My eyes went back to Indigo. "As you were saying?"

She cleared her throat and finished her lemonade off. "Uh yeah. Like I was saying, I didn't have a reason why I hadn't had sex. School was always my main focus. Sure, I dated, but guys brought too many issues. I'm not the one to play games nor do I want to be a part of a roster of women. When I saw that's all the guys were offering in high school, I kept to myself and focused on my studies." This faraway look appeared on her face. "There was one guy I really did like my freshmen year of college. I thought the feelings were mutual but come to find out, he liked my brain more than me. After I realized he was using me, I broke up with him and stayed away from dating."

The server came back and placed everything on the table. Thanking her, I grabbed the black book and grabbed my wallet out my back pocket.

"So why sleep with me?" I placed my card in the book and put it back on the table.

"Honestly." A bashful grin formed on her face and her cheeks heated again. "I just wanted to. Since I first started working for you, I thought you were attractive. I was finishing school and my time working for you was coming to an end. When the opportunity presented itself, I took it. I just didn't think this would be the result." She pointed at her belly and laughed.

"Yeah, me neither. I been fucking since I was fifteen and never got anyone pregnant or close to it. Then suddenly, I'm a dad out of nowhere." I shook my head as the server came for the book.

Indigo grinned. "And I never had sex before but the first time, I get pregnant. Life is funny." She shook her head.

I picked up my glass, finally taking a drink. "Okay, one last question." I sat my glass down. "What's the deal with you and science? Most girls aren't into it, let alone make a career of it."

Her face lit up. "Oh that's not a grand story either. Since I first started learning science in elementary, I became infatuated with it. The older I got, the more I wanted to know. By sixth grade, I knew I wanted to work in the science field when I got older. There are so many different things to know and learn with science, physics, biology, chemical, environmental, and so much more. I was like a sponge soaking it all it. But, eventually, chemical stuck out to me so that's the direction I went. Just like you said you don't see a lot of women take the STEM field on, I wanted to change the narrative. Especially being a young Black woman. I wanted to show there's so much more to us than what society tries to box us into be. If I gotta hold that weight then so be it."

I couldn't lie and say Indigo's explanation didn't impress me. She was more than just a pretty face. She might've only been twenty-seven, but she was a lot more mature than the girls I'd been with in the past. Not to mention, she didn't allow anyone or thing to hinder her goals.

"You're truly one-of-a-kind, Indigo," I complimented.

"You think?" Her head cocked to the side and she smiled softly.

"I do. The women my mom think I'm better with are always superficial. There's no substance to them. Hell, that's with a lot of the women I've dealt with in the past too. You're different, however. You have layers, you're independent, and you work for everything you have regardless of the odds. It's admirable, indeed; sexy even."

"Yeah, well. Thanks, I guess." My cheeks reddened.

When the server came back, she thanked us for coming and walked off. I grabbed the black book and signed the slip then grabbed my card.

"You ready?"

She had packaged up the rest of her food. "Yep."

We headed out the restaurant and headed for my truck. "I enjoyed spending time with you today. It showed me a different side of you," Indigo confessed once we were in the car.

I had to agree with her. At first, I wasn't keen with the thought of her being a permanent fixture in my life, but after talking to her and getting to know her a little better outside of the files I had, I didn't mind her.

"I can say the same about you."

Smiling, she pulled out her phone and tapped the screen. I also noticed she hadn't been on it the whole time we were eating or shopping. Her attention was solely on me. I liked that.

"Anywhere else you want to go?"

With her eyes still on her phone she shook her head. "Nope, now I just want a nap."

I almost suggested we go to New Haven and to my house, but I refrained. We had been together all morning and most of the afternoon. I could drop her off and then stop by MK Hotel and Casino since I was out this way.

Chapter Thirteen

Indigo

The moment I walked into ChocoLUXE, my kids did a happy dance inside me. I'd been craving chocolate and they had the best in the city. Since it was homemade and poured, it never missed. Currently, I wanted one of their smores caramel apples, some chocolate covered strawberries, and the sweet saltiness of their chocolate covered potato chips. My mouth watered at the thought.

"I'm supposed to be on a diet and you bring me in here," Audrey complained.

"I'll make it quick. It's what the babies want." I rubbed my belly and waited in line.

"Yeah, okay." She was on her phone and a smile formed on her face because of whoever she was texting.

"You've been grinning at your phone all day. Who are you texting?"

Audrey was pretty private with her life. Even though we were close, she didn't make anything known unless it was serious. I think it was due to her being an only child.

"Remember the speed dating thing I went to with Charley?"

I nodded and stepped forward when the line moved. "Well I hit it off with one of the guys. We've been seeing each other since."

I waited for her to give me more but she didn't. It was shocking she revealed that much to me.

"And? Are you two dating?"

"We're getting to know each other. We'll see what happens."

"But you like him?" I pushed. I respected Audrey's privacy, but she couldn't just leave me hanging here.

"I do." She nodded and glanced at me with a sly grin. "If things keep going well, I'll bring him around, don't worry."

Finally, it was my turn at the counter. I glanced at the glass case then at Ayame, the owner, and named off everything I wanted.

"Girl, you don't need all that sugar!" Audrey frowned at me.

I waved her off. "It's what the babies want. Plus, I'm not going to eat it all at once."

Going into my crossbody purse, I grabbed my wallet. I was about to grab my debit card when I eyed the card Silas had given me. I hadn't used it since he presented it to me. The purchase was small, but I decided to use it anyways.

"When are you due?" Ayame asked after ringing my things up once she returned.

"October 15th." Looking at her, I remembered something. "You have twins, right?"

A small smile graced her face and nodded. "I do."

I wet my lips. "I'm having twins boys, and although I'm excited, I'm nervous as hell. How was the whole thing if you don't mind me asking." I didn't know Ayame, but I visited ChocoLUXE enough that we had become cordial enough to where I felt comfortable to ask her about her birth.

She snickered and handed me the bag. "The actual labor well hell. I'm not gonna lie. My epidural barely worked and while my first one came out easy, the second one though, that child took his grand ole time." She shook her head. "But now, I wouldn't trade them for anything. They grow up fast and dealing with two babies can get challenging but having their dad to help and the support around me makes it easier."

I took in her information.

The delivery was the main thing that scared me. I didn't take to pain too well and the fact I would have to push two babies out instead of one had me on edge.

"Just try not to get in your head too much. I promise once you set eyes on your babies, it'll all be worth it."

Smiling at her, I thanked her, then me and Audrey made our exit.

"Still can't believe you got knocked up with twins your first time."

"I know. Just my luck, huh," I joked and grabbed the clear container that was filled with the potato chips.

"If you say so." We got to her car.

"Things going well with you and Silas? I admit he wasn't what I was expecting when he showed up at your parents'."

"What were you expecting?"

She started her car. "I don't know. I guess a snob or someone who acted better than all us."

I snickered. "That's the opposite of Silas. And we're good. We've formed some form of friendship, I guess you can call it."

Since my appointment, things with Silas had gotten less tense. He was still having his chef meal prep each week for me and had even sent me a few pictures of things he had gotten or Fiona had got for him, for the babies.

"Mhm. Are you okay with a friendship, honestly?" She side-eyed me.

"Honestly, I am. If he takes care of our kids, I'm not worried about anything else."

That was the truth. Of course, I was still attracted to Silas and missed the sex since I shut it down, but that didn't mean we had to be together. I enjoyed our time together after my appointment. He wasn't as bad to be around like I thought.

My hope was by the time the boys got here, we had become genuine friends.

"Maybe you can find them a step daddy then."

The corner of my mouth ticked. "Now you sound like my sister. With having two newborns, I think dating is at the bottom of my list.

"True, but you've put off dating all your life. It wouldn't hurt to have someone to be with now."

Gnawing on my bottom lip, I turned my attention to the window and watched the passing scenery. Audrey wasn't wrong about that. I had dated, but it never got serious for me. I waited until I was twenty-seven to have sex. Now I was pregnant and my kids' dad didn't even want a relationship with me. Maybe I needed to step out my comfort zone and finally try to take dating more seriously. It's not like I wanted to be alone my whole life.

"Maybe," I spoke lowly while tapping my fingers on my thigh.

It wouldn't hurt to see what's out there. Not sure who would be interested in me with the belly, but once I had my kids, I was open to the idea.

———

I was lounging on my couch when the sound of someone knocking on my door caused me to groan. All day at work my muscles screamed and my back ached. Being on my feet all day while carrying two kids was starting to take a toll on me.

"I'm coming," I mumbled, finally getting up.

One of the twins shifted in my stomach and pressed against my rib. "Easy." I winced, pressing on the spot.

"Who is it?" I asked, grabbing the door handle.

"Pamela Newton." My eyes widened. The last person I was expecting to show up at my house was Silas' mom. My brows furrowed. I had spoken to him earlier and he hadn't mentioned his mom coming here.

Hesitantly, I unlocked the door and pulled it open.

Pamela stood on the other side, looking like she would rather be anywhere than here. Her eyes fell on me with a surly expression on her face.

"Well are you going to invite me in?"

My eyes narrowed and I grabbed my handle tighter, leaning against my door. "It depends. What are you doing here?" I studied her. Not a single hair was out of place in the bun on her head. Her outfit screamed money.

"You are having my only son's children. I think it's time we have a chat." Her eyes fell to my stomach. Protectively, I placed a hand on it.

I wasn't feeling Pamela popping up at my house. Nothing about her was welcoming either. She didn't come across like she was here for a friendly visit.

Stepping back, I opened my door wider. "Come in."

With her head high, she walked past me. Whatever perfume she had on was overbearing and almost caused me to gag and my eyes to water.

Blinking a couple times, I shut the door and turned to face her.

"What can I do for you, Pamela?"

I watched her as she took my house in. Instantly, I noticed the look of displeasure cross her face. Spinning on her heels, she gave me a fake smile.

"Your house is homely." The way she spoke was as if she tasted something bad.

"I think so too. I love my space and don't usually allow bad energy into it."

Amusement passed through her eyes. She eyed my stomach. "Yes, well do you think it's enough to raise kids in. It is rather small." Again, she looked around then back at me.

"I think it's more than enough. Once the twins get older, if I need to move, I'll consider it. But for now, it's perfect for all three of us."

The fake smile on her face dropped and she scoffed. "Seriously, this is a shoebox. You really plan on raising the next generation of Newtons here?"

Crossing my arms and allowing them to rest on stomach, I shifted my weight to the side. My patience was starting to grow thin.

"What brought you here, Pamela? I'm sure it wasn't to insult my house."

A taunting smile split on her face. "What I read about you was true. You're a clever girl." She pressed her lips together. "You aren't the choice I would have liked for my son, but here we are. You are carrying the next generation of Newtons and that's not something we take lightly." Her hands went into her large purse, and she pulled out what looked like a checkbook. "I'm willing to pay you a hundred thousand dollars to sign your rights over to my son and leave my grandkids to have a future."

My mouth parted but I was left speechless by her words. My mouth grew dry and my skin prickled. "Excuse me?" My tongue was heavy in my mouth, but I managed to speak.

"You heard me. Since it's two, I'll even go up to two hundred, but that means you will have no contact with my grandkids nor my son once you give birth." Her eyes went around my house. "Given this place, you could use the money. There's a woman who's willing to accept the twins and start a life with my son. You're the only thing in the way."

As if they could understand the nonsense coming out this woman's mouth, my son's started moving wildly inside me. My mouth slacked and my heart stuttered inside my chest.

Lifting a single brow, I tried to see if this was a joke. When I saw she was serious, I couldn't help but laugh. Bending over, I placed my hands on my knees as my laughing picked up.

Pamela was staring at me like I was crazy but I didn't care. She couldn't seriously think this would work on me.

I wiped the tears that had formed in my eyes and cocked my head to the side. Fire burned inside me. I might have been laughing on the outside but inside I was boiling. The fucking nerve of this woman!

"Are you out of your damn mind?" I blurted out once I gathered myself. My stomach knotted as my sons continued moving frantically.

She stepped back as if I had struck her.

"You come to my house and insult it and then try and buy my kids. Seriously, are you crazy?" My face hardened.

"My grandsons deserve—"

"To be with their mother. I don't care if I don't have the amount of money you and your family has, I'm more than capable of raising my sons and giving them a good life. I don't know who the hell you think you are but you have some nerve coming here and making that crazy ass suggestion."

I stepped back and grabbed my door handle, keeping my eyes on her. "You can take you, your checkbook, and triflin' smelling perfume and get the hell out my house."

Pamela scuffed and tooted her nose up. "Well, I see how this is going to play out. I hoped that we would be able to do this the easy way, but if you want to play ball, so be it." Her checkbook went back into her purse and she started towards me. "Just don't say I didn't try to play nice."

The moment she was through the door, I slammed it shut, hoping I hit her on the way out.

"It's okay, boys," I muttered, rubbing my stomach.

My skin was hot and tight. Adrenaline rushed through my veins.

I didn't know a lot about Pamela, just what Silas had mentioned, but I couldn't believe she would take it as far as to try and buy my kids.

———

My mood had been off all day at work. Last night's visit from Pamela had rattled my nerves, and I wasn't sure how to go about it. Of course, I needed to bring it up to Silas, but I wasn't sure if that would even do anything. He had claimed he handled his mom and then she showed up trying to get me to sell my kids.

Normally, working was relaxing for me, but right now I was too wound up to enjoy what science brought me.

"Indigo," Dr. Foe's voice sounded behind me.

I sat the beaker down and turned to face him. It was our night to close the lab up which typically was great for me. I enjoyed working closely with Dr. Foe, but today I had been distracted, which wasn't smart around chemicals. I was already on certain restrictions due to the fact that I was pregnant, so I couldn't afford to look incompetent.

"Is everything okay? You haven't seemed like yourself today." Concern filled his face.

A smile forced its way on to my face. "Yes, I'm fine. Sorry if I've been distracted. I'm just tired, I guess. Tomorrow I'll be better."

He waved me off. "You did fine today, just like every day. Your work and addition to the team is exceptional. I'm just worried about you. I like to create a space where everyone who works with me feels they can come to me if they need something. If you ever need to talk I'm here."

My skin prickled.

Dr. Foe was so kind. He was seasoned and caring. The way he handled his work was admirable too.

"Let's finish up here so we can head out." He smiled at me, causing me to nod and my smile to grow more genuine.

We spent the next fifteen minutes cleaning the lab up and putting up the samples we were working on.

Like always, Dr. Foe walked me to my car. "Excuse me if this seems inappropriate but I planned on grabbing something to eat. Would you care to join me?"

My heart skated in my chest. I wasn't expecting Dr. Foe to invite me on a date. Well, I didn't really know if it was a date or just two coworkers having dinner together. Still it made my insides warm.

"Sure. I would love to."

"Excellent. Would you like to ride with me and I bring you back to your car? The place I planned to go isn't too far."

"Sure!" I bobbed my head and rubbed my belly. The boys were calm at the moment, thankfully. I'm sure they had picked up on my mood today because they had been causing a ruckus inside me all day.

Dr. Foe led me to the only other car in the parking lot a couple spots down from mine. He stopped at the passenger door and opened it wide for me.

I gave him a soft smile and a shiver shot down my spine when his hand touched my lower back and he helped me inside.

Once I was securely inside, he closed the door and rounded to the driver side.

Trying not to overthink things, I turned and looked at the window while trying to keep my nerves calm.

———

Surprisingly, Dr. Foe was in the mood for Chase's and I wasn't complaining. His restaurant had the best barbeque I ever tasted outside of my daddy's, of course.

So far, we had shared simple small talk. Dr. Foe was unlike a lot of guys around my age; he was able to upkeep a conversation. Currently, we were discussing the samples we had been working on back at the lab.

The moment my food was sat in front of me, I dug into it, practically moaning over the ribs. I wasn't trying to seem like a pig or anything, but the aroma coming from my plate was too demanding for me to eat cute.

Dr. Foe didn't seem to mind, however. He gave me an encouraging smile when I felt embarrassment hit me.

"I thought my wife made the best mac n' cheese, but this place comes close second," he admitted, causing my brows to shoot upwards and my eyes to buck. I dropped my spoon into the bowl of baked beans I was currently working on.

"I didn't know you were married." I nibbled on my bottom lip. He didn't wear a wedding ring and there was no tan line indicating he ever wore one.

A small, toothless smile formed on his face, and his eyes suddenly filled with sadness.

"My wife passed away six years ago from cancer," he admitted.

I gasped.

"Oh my gosh. I'm so sorry."

His face softened. "Thank you. It's the reason I do the kind of research I do. Science has always been a love for me, but when my wife got sick, I made it my mission to try and find a way to help people in the same predicament before they got fatal."

My heart clenched.

"I don't wear my ring because we work with a lot of chemicals, and I fear it may get ruined in the lab."

"That's understandable. What we do could help a lot of people now and in the future."

He nodded. "Unfortunately, my wife was fatal by the time her cancer was found. She got denied clinical trials at the time because of it. Still, she put up a strong fight until the end."

"How long were you married?"

"Fifteen years."

I studied his face, and now that I stared at him, I could see the grief still bouncing around in his eyes. He was smiling but it was somber.

"Wow," I whispered.

"We had great years together that I'll always cherish. If what we do at the lab could help at least one person, I'll be grateful."

I had already had a small crush on Dr. Foe since first laying eyes on him but hearing his story and why he chose to go into our field of study caused me to look at him in a different light.

"Do you have any children?" He shook his head.

"No, I hate to admit it, but we were both too selfish with one another to bring children into the world. It's something I wish we would have reconsidered when we had the time."

I rubbed my stomach. My kids weren't here yet but knowing that a piece of me would be here if anything ever happened to me caused me joy. It pained me that Dr. Foe didn't have that.

"Dr. Foe."

"Greg, please." He gave me a teasing grin.

Bashfully, I grinned. "Greg. What you're doing is admirable. Thank you for sharing it with me."

He waved me off. "No need to thank me. Like I said, I want the lab to be a safe and open place. If anything is ever bothering you, I hope you would feel comfortable enough to come to me and maybe I can help."

I nibbled on my bottom lip; part of me was tempted to admit something *was* bothering me, but I decided against it. The conversation needed to be had with Silas and him alone.

We continued eating, and Greg began asking me about the twins.

Nothing too personal just general questions about my pregnancy and progress.

Dinner was nice and I liked how relaxed it was. Learning more about Dr. Foe had deepened my attraction for him. I felt like a high school girl the way I hung to his words and giggled whenever I thought he said something funny.

My dating experience was limited, but I wouldn't have minded my partner having the same characteristics as Greg.

Chapter Fourteen

Silas

"I can't believe *Mr. I'm never gonna be tied down* is having kids," Caspian joked while I glared at him over the rim of my glass. "Not one, but two! How the hell you manage that?" He chuckled.

"It wasn't something I set out to do." I sat my glass down and grabbed my darts off the table and stood up. Making my way to the dart board, I aimed and threw.

"I'm not gonna lie, this shit is shocking as hell. When you first told us, I thought you were playing," Rhys commented.

Once I threw my last dart, I spun around and headed back for the table. "Go ahead make jokes of it. I've finally come to terms with the idea." I waved both them off.

"Don't listen to them. You're gonna love fatherhood. Watching your kid grow is amazing." Leave it to Lawson to preach how lovely parenthood was. "Hell, I'm tryna convince Zari to have another one. I want her pregnant before the year's over."

I frowned. "Didn't you just have one?"

He shrugged. "My daughter will be a year in three months. I don't want large gaps between my kids."

"Yeah, well, after Indigo has these twins, I'm not having anymore. I never asked for parenthood so Ima be two and done. At least, I'm having boys though. I don't think I would have been able to handle a girl."

"What's going on with you and Indigo, anyways?" Rhys questioned.

"What do you mean? Nothing. We get along well, but that's it."

"She's hot," Caspian commented. "If I was you, I would have locked her down the moment I found out she was pregnant."

I mugged him. Yes, Indigo was attractive. She was fine as hell, actually, but that didn't mean I wanted to hear another nigga comment on it.

"You know I'm not the relationship type."

"That shit still doesn't make sense to me. You got to grow up one day, Si." My mug turned to Lawson.

"What's that supposed to mean?"

"All that bouncing from bed to bed was cool when we were in our twenties, but we're all men now. We own successful businesses, we're wealthy, and in our thirties. Still behaving like some young-minded kid isn't how you should move."

"Relationships aren't for everyone. Just because you're someone who wanted it doesn't mean it's for everyone. It doesn't make me young-minded either."

Hell, it'd been a while since I even been with a woman. The last one I slept with was Indigo right before she let me know it was the last time.

"You're right." He shrugged. "Relationships aren't for everyone, but you're about to have your own family. The girl is giving you two kids, don't you think she and the kids deserve some kind of stability. I'm not even saying dive right in, but you shouldn't be so resistant."

"I don't think Silas should have to be with the girl because she's having his babies," Caspian countered.

"Agreed, but what's stopping him? From what you've mentioned, she doesn't seem like she's trying to change you or use you. What's keeping you from letting your guard down with her? Even if it's not with her, don't you think eventually, you're gonna want to settle down with someone. Yo can't do that while you're still holding onto your childhood. You say you hate the control your parents had over you, but from where I'm standing, it seems like they still have it." He tossed the rest of his drink back and grabbed his darts, heading for the board.

My eyes dropped down to the table and my tongue poked the inside of my cheek. Leave it to Lawson to be the voice of reason.

I had fought hard to get from under my parents' control and rules. Was I truly still allowing them to influence me?

My brows furrowed. Nah, Lawson was just being Lawson.

The conversation shifted but was still hanging heavy on my mind.

"By the way, this weekend we're having a small gathering at the house. You guys are invited. Silas, you can bring Indigo too," Lawson let us know when he got back to the table.

"What's the occasion?" I questioned.

"I'm about to open my second hotel since taking over as CEO, and Zari felt like we should celebrate that and the success of the one in Butter Ridge. Some place called Chase's is catering."

"Ima grab another drink," I spoke up and turned to leave the table, still stuck on Lawson's words.

The second I got to the bar, my phone vibrated. Pulling it out, I saw it was Indigo.

Speak of the devil.

A couple notifications came through from my betting app as well. I got the bartender's attention and made my order before turning my attention back to my phone.

———

I was in the middle of reviewing some paperwork when the buzzer on my desk went off, gaining my attention.

"Mr. Newton, Indigo Jenkins is here to see you."

I glanced at the time. Indigo had texted me earlier, letting me know she needed to speak to me, and since I was planning on being at the office all day, I let her know to come by here. What I didn't expect was for time to go by as quickly as it did.

122

I pressed the button. "Send her in." I signed the paper in front of me and when the door opened, I set the forms to the side.

She waddled inside, her skin glowing, face chunky, and locs pulled into a half-up half-down style. It had only been a few days since I laid eyes on her but it looked like her stomach had grown more in just that short period of time.

Indigo made her way to my desk with a pinched expression on her face. I tilted my head and noted the tension in her body.

She took a seat in one of the chairs and glared at me. "I'm assuming this isn't a friendly visit," I started off.

"You told me you spoke to your mom."

I narrowed my eyes. "I did." The last thing I expected was this conversation to be centered around my mom.

"And what was said?"

I shrugged. "It went. Why?" My hands folded on top of my desk and I leaned forward.

"Well obviously not well because she came by my house the other day!" That was news to me. I wasn't even aware my mother knew where Indigo lived, but then Pamela Newton was a resourceful woman.

"And I'm guessing by how you're acting something happened?"

"She tried to buy my babies!" Her voice squeaked as it heightened.

My nose scrunched and a scold covered my face. "She did what?"

"You heard me. She offered me money to give you my babies and disappear when they're born. I don't know how your family operates but in mine, we just don't sell our kids to the highest bidder. I don't give a damn if I'm not rich. I deserve and *will* raise my kids and no one is going to take them from me! I will die before I—"

"Indigo!" My hand went up and voice boomed, shutting her rant down. Her mouth snapped shut and her eyes squinted. "I have no plans of taking the boys from you nor was I aware of my mother coming to see you."

I scratched the back of my neck as it grew warm. I didn't like seeing Indigo upset, especially at the cause of my mother. Leave it to Pamela to go behind my back and do something crazy.

"I will speak to my mother again. She won't bother you further."

"You said that last time." Her voice was tight and her was body still tense.

"And I thought I got through to her but it seems I'll have to have another conversation with her. I'll handle it."

I could see she didn't believe me. Her orbs were guarded.

"One of my friends is hosting a gathering at his house this weekend. He invited me and told me to bring you along."

"What?" Her face scrunched. "Why?"

"Apparently, my friends want to get to know you better."

"They know about me?"

"Well you are having my kids. Of course, they know about you."

The look of confusion didn't leave her face. "Yeah but…" her voice trailed off.

"Look, ignore whatever my mom told you. I told you I don't give a fuck about all that social standing bullshit. Just because I have more money doesn't mean I'm better than you or anyone else. My friends aren't like that either."

Indigo tapped her fingers on her thigh and tapped her foot. "I'm gonna go because free food sounds like heaven to me right now. The moment I feel uncomfortable or like I'm being judged, I'm leaving."

"You have nothing to worry about." She bored a heated glare at me.

"Handle your mom, Silas. If she approaches me again all gloves are off. I won't allow anyone to threaten to take my children from me, I don't care who they are."

"It'll be handled." I picked my phone up. "Have you eaten? I can have some food brought here for you since you're here."

"I'm gonna be a thousand pounds by the time I deliver. Everyone wants to feed me," she muttered, causing me to raise a brow. "I can eat."

I nodded and unlocked my phone.

Indigo hung around my office for a little over an hour once the food arrived before she left. I had an off-site meeting to attend that Fiona had popped in and reminded me of.

As much as I wanted to blow the meeting off and go confront my mom, I couldn't. I was cool around Indigo but inside, I was boiling.

My mom had taken things too far this time and it was time I finally shut her and her actions down, for good.

———

I had tunnel vision as I stormed through my parents' house, already knowing they were in the family room. The moment I left work, I made my way over. Indigo's confession had me tense and burning since she left my office.

"Mother!" I called out when I laid eyes on her.

Her head turned from the TV to me. "Silas? Honey, I wasn't aware you were coming over. I hope you're here to apologize for you previous behavior."

My skin prickled as if ants were crawling on it. My blooded heated and felt like a raging river in my veins.

My mom had done some underhanded things in my life, but this was the lowest.

"What gives you the right to offer Indigo money for my kids!" I boomed with my hands balled at my side.

Mom stared at me blankly. "Silas, that hussy is not fit to raise my grandchildren. They are Newtons and deserve to be raised as such."

My hands clenched tighter. I noticed my dad was nowhere to be found tonight, he was more than likely on a business trip.

"You don't get to make that decision! My entire life you've controlled how I live and tried to mold me into who you think I should be, and it stops now! I refuse to let my kids anywhere near you and have you corrupt them."

"Corrupt them?" She cocked her head back. "I'm trying to save them! That woman has nothing to offer your kids. Did you see where she lives? My closet is bigger than that."

"That woman is gonna be a better mother than you ever were! Not only is she intelligent and caring, but she comes from a great background, and she'll give my kids the love a parent should!" I bit down on my back teeth and rolled my neck between my shoulders. My nose flared. "I'm going to tell you one time and one time only, stay the hell away from Indigo and my kids. They will have nothing to do with you or your fucked-up way of thinking. I'm washing my hands with you!" I barely recognized my voice as it came out in a low growl like tone.

My last set of words caused a gasp to leave my mom's mouth, and she grabbed her chest. "How dare you speak to me in that manner!"

"How dare you try and pay my kids' mom to leave them! Do you not realize how fucked-up that is!" My heart pounded loudly in my ears and my chest grew tight.

A look I couldn't decipher appeared on my mom's face.

"Maybe you need to see what your kids' mom has been up to! Maybe then you'll agree with me," she said in snarky tone.

My brows bunched together and mouth turned upside down.

Silently, I watched her reach over and grab an envelope that was next to her. She stood and made her way over to me. "I planned on dropping these off to you, but since you're here." She held the envelope out once she reached me.

Dropping my eyes down, I stared at it curiously. "Take it. See the kind of woman you're disrespecting your mother for."

Slowly, I reached out and grabbed the large yellow envelope. I quickly ripped it open and saw photos inside.

"What is this?" I pulled them out, allowing the envelope to fall at my feet. My eyes squinted as I flicked through them, seeing they were of Indigo and some guy.

"While you're here defending her honor, that woman is dating a whole 'nother man. Is that the kind of woman you want to raise your kids? One that thinks it's acceptable to date while pregnant?"

Ignoring her last sentiment, I continued to flip through the pictures. Whoever the guy was, was older than Indigo, that was clear. In the current photo I was looking at, she was staring at the guy with a dazzled look on her face.

"How did you get these?" I brought my bottom lip between my teeth and shifted my eyes to meet my mom's.

Her arms crossed. "Do you think I wouldn't make sure our legacy was protected? I hired a private investigator to follow her. Since you decided to go against my wishes and impregnant some random hussy, I needed to know who we were dealing with."

"You had no right to do this!" The photos shook in my hand. "This is what I'm talking about, you overstep! I'm not a child, Mother! I don't need you inserting yourself in my life!"

My eyes dropped to the pictures. A sharp stabbing sensation shot through my chest. My stomach stirred.

"I did this for you!"

"No! You did this for *you!* This is it! This is the final straw. Fire your investigator and mind your damn business!" I dropped the pictures.

I needed to get out of here. I wasn't tryna disrespect my mom, but I was sick of her shit. You would have thought I slapped my mom the way her head snapped back. Her mouth opened but no words fell from it.

Turning on my heels, I rushed out the room to the front of the house.

Chapter Fifteen

Indigo

B elieve it or not, I didn't do well with new people. It wasn't like I was shy or anything, I just didn't know how to handle large social settings. Thankfully, my sister and cousin were able to accompany me to this cookout Silas invited me to. After what happened with his mom, I was on edge about meeting anyone else in his world. When I voiced that and mentioned bringing my sister and cousin, he didn't shut it down.

"Damn, this house is nice as fuck," Charley complimented, wide-eyed.

We drove through the gate up the long driveway.

"What does this guy do again?" Audrey glanced over at me from the driver's seat.

"He's the CEO of the MK hotel and casinos." This time, her eyes enlarged.

"Shit, he's loaded. *Issa Vibe* magazine just did an article on him and his wife. His hotel was also just featured in *Word Weekly*. It's the most successful growing business Butter Ridge Falls has seen in while according to *Word Weekly*."

While *Issa Vibe* was more a regional magazine that focused on lifestyle, culture, entertainment and the latest news, *Word Weekly* was dedicated to everything around Butter Ridge Falls. Since Audrey worked there, I wasn't shocked that she knew this information.

"He was in Forbes too. *Be Bold* also did a spotlight on him for that show *Melanin and Wealthy.*"

"Go ahead and give us his biography too," Charley joked, causing me to snickered.

Once Audrey threw the car in park, she flicked her off. "Whatever. As a journalist, it's my job to stay informed." I removed my seat belt and turned back to the house. It was bigger than any I had ever been in. I could only imagine what the inside looked like from the well-groomed landscape.

"Do we go in or what?" Charley leaned into the front and questioned.

"Hold on." Grabbing my phone, I sent Silas a text letting him know we had arrived.

"Girl you better lock down rich baby daddy and get him to buy you a house like this."

I turned and frowned at my sister. "Why the hell would I need something this big? And stop calling him that!"

She rolled her eyes and waved me off. "Because you're about to have two kids. Your house is nice, but don't you think you need more room especially once they get bigger? Not to mention, he can afford it so why not."

My stomach flipped as I thought about what she just said, and it made me recall Pamela's words.

"All I'm saying is, he has the money, and you're about to have two kids. There's no point for you three to be all on top of each other if you don't have to be." Her shoulders lifted.

"I hate to agree with her, but something bigger would be more circumstantial. You just have a two bedroom right now too, don't you think a three bedroom would be better?"

Bringing my bottom lip between my teeth, I nibbled on it and thought it out. I planned on moving when the time came, but I planned on waiting until the twins got a little bigger.

My phone vibrating in my lap gained my attention. When I

glanced down, I saw it was Silas letting me know he was at the front door. Looking up, I saw him waiting, gesturing us in a c'mon motion.

"There goes Silas," I mentioned, opening my door and grabbing my bucket purse.

My hand went to my back as I waddled to the door. "You okay?" Silas asked once I got closer.

"Yeah, cars sit low so getting in and out of them are kind of a hassle. I'm fine though." I stood straight. "This house is beautiful."

He scanned me over. "Yeah, Lawson went all out when he had it built. Hello ladies," he greeted Charley and Audrey.

"Hey!" they both greeted.

"Follow me." Silas grabbed my hand and helped me up the two steps then placed his hand on the small of my back.

"Damn."

"Shit," sounded from behind us. My mouth parted and eyes widened as I took in the inside of the house. It was gorgeous.

"How many people live here?" I glanced at Silas.

"Three. Lawson, his wife, and daughter." Heading through the hallway, I glanced at the others as we passed them.

"How many bedrooms does this place have?" Charley asked.

"I believe four."

"Four? That's all in this big ass house!"

"Charley!" I stopped and glanced over my shoulders.

She tossed her hands up. "My bad."

Silas found her outburst amusing. "There are a lot of other rooms that take up space." We got to the large kitchen and he led us to the glass sliding doors.

"Wow, even the backyard is gorgeous." Lawson's yard had a patio lounge area where all the guests were currently and an outdoor fireplace with an attached grill. In the yard a few steps away was a pool and hot tub.

I turned to face my girls, and they looked just as amazed while taking in the yard.

Silas led us over to where his friends were. I took in account there were four other girls and three guys. The moment we reached them, one of them noticed us.

"Hey!" He grinned, his eyes bouncing to each of us.

The woman hugged up at his side also looked over.

Silas looked at me. "That's Lawson and his wife, Zarinah."

"Nice to meet you. Thank you for inviting us." I smiled at the couple.

"Don't mention it. You're a part of the crew now," Lawson mentioned.

Out the corner of my eyes, I saw Silas's jaw twitch at his statement. He cleared his throat. He started pointing at people as if Lawson didn't speak. "This is Aspen, Lawson's sister, Kimmie, Inayah, Rhys, and Caspian. Everyone, Indigo and her sister, Charley and cousin, Audrey."

Everyone shared their welcomes.

"There's food on the tables over there if you guys are hungry." Zarinah pointed. "I got cornhole, and we were getting ready to set teams up to play if you're interested as well. Oh and there's drinks at the bar both alcoholic and nonalcoholic over there."

Damn, these people were really loaded.

My stomach stirred at the mention of food. "I can eat."

"Of course you can," Charley joked. I turned and flicked her off while laughing with her.

"Silas, take her to the food," Lawson encouraged.

"C'mon." His hand was still on the small of my back and he led me over to the where the tables were closer to the doors we just exited.

"Ooooo is that Chase's?" I observed the logo on the containers. My inside's danced.

"I'm guessing you like this place?" A smile ticked on his face.

"I do! It's one of my favorite places." I grabbed a plate and noticed my sister and Audrey had followed and did the same.

Going down the line, I eagerly added food to my plate. We walked over to the bar, and I saw there was a cooler. Since my hands were full, Silas opened it for me. "Can you grab me a sweet tea?"

He did as I mentioned and led us back to his friends. My sister and Charley had made themselves comfortable. I wasn't shocked; it was easy for them to adapt to new people. They were in conversation with Kimmie and Inayah. I looked at them and noticed Kimmie looked familiar.

"So Indigo, how are you liking pregnancy?" Zarinah questioned after a while. The guys were currently in the yard setting up the cornhole things for us, conversing among themselves.

Using a napkin to wipe my mouth, I swallowed my food before speaking. "Oddly, I love it. I hate how tired and hungry I always am, but besides that everything is good. Oh, I could do without the weight gain too."

She snickered. "I know that feeling. I was sick my whole first trimester and the beginning of my second. My weight gain came towards the end of my pregnancy. Thankfully, I was mainly baby."

"Is your daughter here?" I looked around, not seeing a baby.

She shook her head. "No my in-laws have her for the day."

"Which I'm upset about. I miss my baby." Aspen pouted.

Zarinah rolled her eyes. "You just saw her yesterday."

Aspen scrunched her nose. "What does that mean? My brother always acts like it'll kill him to part for her longer than a day. He's so stingy with her."

Zarinah snickered. "You know that's his whole world, right? Why not just have a baby of your own," Kimmie suggested.

Aspen waved her off. "No thank you. I love babies I can give back. I'm not ready to be no one's permanent caretaker."

I studied Aspen; confidence and assurance dripped from her.

"Yeah, Aspen gives rich auntie vibes. Not mama vibes," Inayah mentioned.

"Exactly, don't push motherhood on me." She flicked her hair over her shoulders. The four were obviously close.

Zarinah rolled her eyes. "Anyways, pregnancy is exciting overall. Feeling your baby grow, watching it. Well in your case them, you're having twins, right?"

"Twins!" Both Kimmie and Aspen stared at me in shock.

I rubbed my belly. "Yep. Two-for-one special in here." I giggled.

"Damn. I would lose my mind."

"Kimmie!" Zarinah chastised.

"What, I'm just saying!" She shrugged.

"It's fine." I grinned. "I thought the same in the beginning too. It was a surprise for me, but now I've come to terms with it. I'm looking forward to meeting both of them."

"Well, I for one can't wait!" Charley leaned in and went to rub my stomach.

"Stop!" I slapped her hand away.

"Now that I don't miss." Zarinah laughed. "People always wanting to touch my stomach was not fun."

"And my sister doesn't respect personal space."

Charley waved me off. "We're sisters. Those are my nephews. What space do I need?" She rolled her eyes.

I shook my head, knowing there was no point in trying to explain. "Anyways. What do all you ladies do?"

"I work legal for MK Hotel and Casino," Aspen informed.

"Massage therapist," both Zarinah and Inayah said.

"I own Glow." My head snapped to Kimmie.

"That's why you look so familiar. I think I've come to you for a facial or at least your business."

She grinned. "Probably. I've been up and running for a few years now. What about you guys?" Her eyes bounced between us.

"I'm a VA for a couple different people," my sister let them know.

"Journalist." I had almost forgotten Audrey was here. She had been quietly eating in the background, which I wasn't shocked because although she was good in new environments, she was observant too. That's what made her such a great journalist.

"I'm a scientist."

All four eyes shot open. "Scientist? Like a real one?" Aspen asked.

My face crinkled before laughing. "Uhm, yeah? I work at a clinic in Butter Ridge Falls that focuses on genetic testing and gene therapy."

"I don't even know what the hell that means," she mumbled.

"It's okay. A lot of people don't. Basically, I study ways to help cure diseases, correct defective genes, and study genetics. Things like that."

"Damn, you must be smart then." That was Kimmie.

"Hell yeah, my sister is the smartest person I've ever met."

I blushed. "Charley, please."

"What, you are!" She looked offended. "When it comes to science and math, my sister knows her shit. She can run with the best of them."

One thing I loved about my sister was how she always hyped me up with my career choice. Where most people might've been intimated by it, she wasn't. She always made sure to brag on me.

"That's amazing!" Zarinah's face lit up.

"Thank you." The guys had come back over, letting us know we could start the game.

"Silas, why didn't you tell us how smart your kids' mom was? Baby, did you know she was a scientist?" Zarinah looked at her husband who pulled her up and in his arms. He kissed the top of her head.

"I was aware. Silas mentioned it in passing."

Silas turned his attention to me. Something I couldn't make out flashed through his eyes. "Honestly, I'm still getting used to it myself." He grabbed the back of his neck. We held each other's stare and my heart fluttered.

"Okay, well, let's pick teams so we can play. Are you joining?" Zarinah asked me after a few seconds.

I shook my head. "I'm good. I am going to get another plate if that's okay."

"Oh go ahead. There's more than enough. Shall we, guys?" She looked at everyone else.

While the group headed for the yard where the cornhole was set up, Silas surprised me by taking a seat next to me.

"I want to apologize for my mom's behavior," he blurted out. I wasn't expecting that to come out his mouth. "I went and spoke to her and made sure to let her know her actions were out of line."

I swallowed hard. "Thank you. I know you can't dictate what your mom does, but I appreciate you having my back."

He cracked his fingers and looked out in the yard. "At the end of the day, you and the twins are my responsibility. I might not have asked for this, but that doesn't mean I'm going to let anyone cause you any discomfort either. She was wrong, and I had no choice but to let her know that."

My eyes dropped to my almost empty plate. The twins were moving wildly in my stomach. "I think the twins like the idea of you defending us." I ran my fingers over the area the movement was.

His eyes lit up and dropped. He went to touch but paused, giving me a questioning look.

I grabbed his hand and placed it on the movement. "This still is crazy to me." His head shook. "You really got two humans inside you."

"I know right." I dragged my tongue over my lips. "It seems like time's getting closer and closer to their arrival. It feels like just yesterday I learned I was pregnant, now here I am a little over halfway through."

Silas' touch on my stomach was gentle as he stroked it. The hair on the back of my neck raised. He gazed at me with a soft expression on his face.

"Are you finally excited about becoming a dad? I know you don't want to be tied down or whatever."

He wet his lips and blinked a couple times. "Oddly, I believe I am. I don't know what happened but after learning the sex and seeing them again, I've become more accepting of them. More open to being a father. I also want to be the opposite of the parents I grew up with." His jaw clenched.

My hand moved over to his leg and rested on top his knee. "I believe you will be. You're a good guy, Silas."

He smirked. "I don't know about all that, but I'm trying." His answer confused me. Yeah he was a little demanding and controlling, but I got nothing but good vibes from him.

"Your friends seem nice. Not at all what I was expecting," I replied instead.

I watched as everyone joked and talked in the yard. The current game seemed to be growing intense.

"Yeah, they're a good group. I've known Law and Caspian since we were kids and we met Rhys in high school."

"So you guys been friends for a long time, wow. I never really had girlfriends. It's always just been me, my sister, and cousin."

"You guys are a good group. You can tell you grew up close."

I grinned. "Yeah, Audrey has always been like another sister rather than a cousin. Her parents worked a lot, and she's an only child so she spent a lot of time at my house."

"I always wished I had siblings." His shoulders fell forward slightly. I don't think he even knew he was still rubbing my stomach, but I didn't mention it. Oddly, it was comforting to me.

"My parents never wanted more than one kid and didn't see the point after their first born was a boy. But being the center of all their attention was a lot, and I hated it. I'm glad to have befriended Caspian and Law because it gave me an escape I desperately needed. Whenever I could I was at one of their houses."

"Are you and your dad not close either?" Since I had only met his mom, I knew how she was, but I didn't know anything about Silas' dad. He never spoke on them individually either.

"Nah, my dad was always about business. He owns an international shipping company that's been in the family for years. He traveled a lot for work and was the background parent. While my mom was always demanding with what she required, he only really voiced his opinions when he felt it was necessary."

His words made my chest ache. I couldn't imagine not being close to my parents or having the security in them that I did. They were always warm and loving to me and all my siblings.

"I'm sorry. I couldn't imagine growing up like that." His shoulders raised. This time he moved his hand from my stomach and ran it down his mouth.

"No need to apologize. It's something I've come to accept. My family was never close growing up. Everyone pretty much looked out for themselves."

I chewed the inside of my cheek. "Well now you have the chance to change that. I grew up close to my family and that's how I plan on raising the twins. I would love for you to be a part of it."

His head cocked to the side, and he studied me with his dark orbs. He pulled his brows together and pressed his lips in a straight line.

"After the conversation with my mother, I had to step back and re-evaluate some things. Like I mentioned, I didn't grow up close to my parents or anyone else in my family. Aunts and uncles were limited and didn't live close, both my grandparents are gone so my family interaction is limited. After being at your family barbeque and realizing how different our families are, I know that my kids are going to have a warm and fulfilling life. The total opposite from what I grew up with." A small grin formed on his mouth. "My mom was wrong. Trying to pay you off so that you would leave our kids and allow them to be raised how I was is unacceptable, and I'll never allow that to happen. I know you're going to raise them to be great and give them the nurturing kids need and love growing up. My parents know nothing about raising a child and how to be a real parent. I have no doubt that you'll be everything the twins need."

This time, I grabbed one of his hands and enveloped it in mine. They were warm and larger than my own. "*We'll* be everything they need. You keep mentioning me as a parent, but Silas, I have no doubt you're going to be just as great."

He snorted. "With my background, I'm not so sure. I can run a business, no problem, but raising kids well..." His voice trailed off. It was then I saw the insecurities within him surfacing.

"You're not going to be anything like your parents if that's what you're afraid of, Silas. I have faith in you. This will be trial and error for both of us and we'll get some things wrong, but I have no doubt you'll be a great dad."

"And what makes you think that? After all you know about me and how I grew up. Hell from what I've shown you. What makes you think that?"

This time the smile on my face grew and my hands tightened around his. "Simple. Because you know how you don't want your kids to grow up and how not to raise them. I'm sure that alone with help mold you into the perfect dad for our sons."

Chapter Sixteen

Silas

"You like her," Lawson mentioned next to me.

The gathering had been a success. Indigo and her family hit it off with the rest of the girls. They had all been attached at the hip, talking about God knows what. Every time I snuck a peek at Indigo, she was smiling and in high spirits.

"Yeah, what's not to like."

He smirked and shook his head. His hands went into his pockets. "Nah, I mean *like* her. You haven't kept your eyes off her since she arrived."

"She's around a bunch of people she hasn't met before. I'm just making sure she's straight."

Lawson shook his head. "You don't have to deny you have feelings for her, Si. No one's gonna judge you. From what I've seen you did good. She has a good head on her shoulders, and she seems genuine."

"Good head on her shoulders?" I snorted. "You sound like a proud parent." I chuckled, turning my attention back to Indigo. Just as I focused on her, she turned her attention to me. The smile on her face kicked up. My heart responded, thumping hard and steady against my chest.

"Ima have to go check that Chase's place out. Their peach cobbler is good as hell." Caspian walked up, smacking on the cobbler on his plate.

"Take the rest home. I doubt anyone here finishes it," Lawson let him know.

"You ain't gotta tell me twice." He shoved his spoon in his mouth.

I picked my beer bottle up and brought it to my mouth. It had been a while since I got together with the guys outside The Raven. I glanced at my phone and noticed the betting app I used had notified me of my winnings from the games I'd betted on.

I had been slowing down this week, being that there was a horse race coming up that I planned on betting big at.

Rhys had made his way back over to us. "Today was a good day," he expressed, sitting on one of the couches with his legs gapped. He pulled his phone out and tapped it a couple times.

"It was, wasn't it?" The girls had come over. Zari didn't hesitate to slide into her husband's lap. His arms instantly went around her.

Everyone crowded around, taking places on the couches. Indigo found a spot next to me. She yawned, and I wasn't sure if she noticed but her body gravitated towards me. It slacked back against me.

"You a'right?" I dipped my head and whispered in her ear.

She glanced up at me. It was clear fatigue had settled in the pockets of her eyes. "I'm good, I had a nice time today. Thanks for inviting me."

"I'm glad you're getting along with everyone."

I moved my arm so it was now wrapped around her, and I pulled her closer to me. Her head rested on my chest.

"Well, I be damn," Caspian's voice sounded.

"I wouldn't believe it if I didn't see it." Rhys followed up.

When I glanced at the two, I noticed all eyes were on us. "What?" My mouth turned upside down.

Smiles twitched on their mouths. "You just look comfortable."

"Especially for something you claim you don't want." My eyes dropped back down to Indigo. Her eyes were now closed and her breathing evened out.

"I'm glad my cousin is comfortable with you," Audrey spoke up.

I glanced at her and narrowed my eyes. I couldn't get a read of the girl. She was quiet but social at the same time. It was like she was always in the background though, waiting and watching.

"I did some research and the further she gets in her pregnancy, the less energy she'll have, especially carrying two. It's my job to make sure she's comfortable." My hand ran down her bare skin.

"Silas puts on a big front but deep down, he's an affectionate guy. You ladies have nothing to worry about," Lawson let them know, causing me to cut my eyes in his direction.

"I don't need a spokesperson."

He waved me off. "I think he's a good guy too." Indigo's eyes fluttered open. She yawned and went to sit up, but I kept my grip around her tight.

"You're good, relax," I let her know when she looked at me in confusion.

I couldn't put my finger on what it was but I enjoyed having her close to me like this. I didn't like seeing the distress my mother caused her and then the photos I was shown popped in my mind. I shouldn't have been shocked that someone else had her attention; Indigo was a catch. She might've been new to dating, but it was obvious she wouldn't accept anything less than what she deserved. Sadly, I was too selfish to think of another male in my kids' life, or hers if I was being honest.

"I think you two look good together. Even if you don't get together, having a healthy relationship is good for your kids," Zari mentioned.

"Here goes the love guru," Kimmie joked, causing her, Inayah, and Aspen to laugh.

"Whatever, I'm just saying!" She snuggled closer into Lawson.

I fought the urge to push Indigo away. It wasn't as if I had an issue with intimacy or anything, but the thought of being tied down made my skin itch.

The evening continued and by the end, I was glad I invited Indigo.

Everyone was headed for their cars in the front of the house when Indigo stopped walking and faced me. "Can I go with you?" she asked, shocking me.

I stared down at her. "Are you sure?"

Her eyes shifted over to where Charley and Audrey were waiting before she nodded her head. "Yeah, I have some things I want to talk to you about and we really didn't get to here."

Tomorrow was Sunday, meaning it was a free day for me. Since I didn't plan to do anything too major, I didn't mind her joining me.

"If you're sure, it's fine with me."

"Hold on." She turned to her family. "I'm going to leave with Silas. You guys can go ahead."

The two of them shared a look. "Okay. Call us later!" They climbed inside the car.

I led her over to where my car was, thinking about what she said earlier. "If I would have known you were gonna leave with me, I would have drove my truck."

"It's fine." She shrugged.

"Indigo, don't allow Silas to keep you away!" Caspian called out, passing by us.

"I won't." She smiled over her shoulder as I held the door open for her to hop inside.

Once she was safely in the car, I rounded to the driver side.

"I wasn't sure what to expect when we got here. Part of me was nervous your friends would look down on us," Indigo confessed when we were on the road. I lived about fifteen minutes away from Lawson.

"Why did you think that?" I snuck a peek at her.

She shrugged. "I don't know how it moves in your world."

I chuckled. "We're normal people, Indigo, just because we have money doesn't make us any better than anyone."

"Yeah, well most rich people don't agree." I chewed the inside of my jaw. That was true. In fact, most people I grew up around were who she was describing.

"I never surrounded myself with those kinds of people so you won't have to worry about that." I despised those kinds of people who in fact, reminded me too much of my closeminded parents. "Besides, you and Zarinah are from the same city and her friends too. No one was gonna look down on you."

She tapped her fingers on the door frame. "Can I ask you something?" Her head turned to face me.

I nodded, encouraging her to go ahead. "After seeing Lawson's house it made me wonder why don't you have one of your own. I mean why live in a condo instead of something like that?"

Licking my lips and pressing them together for a moment, I thought how to answer her. "My parents have a large house kind of like that. They were always on the go and so most of the time, it was only me and the staff. When they were around, they were always dictating how and what I did. I don't know... I guess that made me despise having all that space. I was lonely growing up outside of when I was with my friends, even still at home it was just me.

My condo brings me comfort. I have my space, yet it's not overly large. I don't have that empty feeling I used to have when I was a kid. With it being just me there's no need to have a large house."

I glanced at her then back at the street. "Makes sense, but didn't you ever think you would have a family?"

"No, I didn't. I didn't want to be boxed in."

"And a family would do that."

My grip on wheel tighten. "In a sense. At least that's what I used to believe."

Silence filled the air around us.

Once we got my condo and pulled into my parking garage, I hopped out the car and walked over to help her out.

"Cars really don't do you well, huh?" I noted when she struggled to get up.

"Thanks to the extra cargo I'm carrying, no." She snickered.

We headed for the elevator and she made sure to grab the to-go plates she had made.

"I know I mentioned I wanted to talk, but I'm exhausted. Can we wait 'til the morning?" Indigo asked once we were inside my condo. I set the alarm and inhaled the lemon scent. Thankfully, the new housekeeper had been doing a good job.

"Yeah, go ahead. I'm going to go into my office." I had a poker game calling my name.

She gave me a soft grin. "Okay. Do you mind giving me a shirt to sleep in, since I don't have clothes here?"

My eyes scanned her body over. "Yeah, follow me."

Removing my shoes, I headed for my bedroom. "Let me put this in the fridge," she called out behind me.

I looked around my condo as I headed for my room. The big open space gave me a sense of freedom, it also made think though. Since I would be having two kids running around eventually, maybe a bigger place might be needed.

Once in my room, I went to my dresser and grabbed a shirt. "This should fit." I turned and handed it to Indigo.

"Thank you." Her eyes shifted around my bedroom then fell to me. "Well Ima go lay down."

I watched as she turned and tottered off.

Wanting to get comfortable myself, I undid my button up and yanked my shorts down.

"Oh, I forgot to mention I—" Spinning around, Indigo's voice trailed off. I was only in my boxers now and her eyes dropped to my dick.

"I, uh, never mind." She blinked slowly.

One corner of my mouth ticked up and I raised a brow. Quickly, she spun around and darted away from my room, causing me to chuckle.

I changed into some sweats, leaving my shirt off then walked back into my living room to pour myself a drink, and then head to my office to spend a few hours getting lost in some cards.

————

The next day, I ordered both me and Indigo breakfast and made sure it was there before she woke up. I had spent an hour on my treadmill before showering and now I was sitting on my couch with my laptop looking over my earnings.

This morning, I had made a few calls that hopefully would work out in my favor as well.

By the time Indigo was up and fed, I was up and ready for the day.

"Thanks for letting me borrow some clothes," she mentioned. I had loaned her some basketball shorts and a shirt. Her weight gained made them fit her perfectly.

"No problem." She walked over and sat next to me.

"So…" She started folding her hands in her lap. "Do you think I can see the condo downstairs?"

To say her words shocked me was an understatement. Last she mentioned, she didn't want to move.

"I thought you weren't interested." She shrugged.

"I wasn't but my sister made a point yesterday. My townhouse is nice, but these condos have more space. With two kids it'll be easier to maneuver, not to mention it's a three-bedroom opposed to my two."

My head bobbed. I planned on presenting the condo as an option again before the twins got here but hearing her bring it up herself made me happier.

"Well, let's go see it." I stood up then turned to help her.

We headed for the front door. I shoved my phone in my pocket and grabbed the set of keys on the key ring on the wall.

The first thing I did when I checked this place out was buy the building. One thing I valued was privacy and didn't want strangers having access to my space. The downstairs condo had been empty since I moved in. It was the size of mine minus the terrace and pool.

I stayed in the living room while Indigo gave herself the tour. Since the layout was close to mine and she was familiar with it, I knew she didn't need me.

"This is beautiful. I can't lie." She turned towards the large bay window and looked out. "There's more space than my townhouse as well." The silence between us made my heart beat sound louder.

"Is the offer still available?" She spun around and her eyes bored into me.

"If you want it." I tried to keep my voice leveled. Even though I would rather move her things in here and make her stay, I was trying to give her an option. She mentioned she didn't like me trying to control her life and it was hard but I was being considerate of that.

"Okay." Her head bobbed. "I'll take it. At least for now. But I want to pay rent."

"No." I shut her down. Her brows squinted.

"I don't want a handout or for it to seem like—"

"I said no. I own the building; no extra money goes into staying here. I'm not going to charge the mother of my kids to live here. I'll have make some calls and have a company get your stuff moved."

She blinked.

"Just like that?"

"Just like that."

For a second, hesitancy passed through her face. "I don't want it as if you're taking care of me."

"I'm taking care of my kids and making sure they're good."

She nibbled on the corner of my bottom lip. "I want you to respect my privacy. That means not coming and going as you please." Her stare became intense.

My heart throbbed. "Are you seeing anyone at the moment?"

Confusion filled her face. "What? No. What does that have to do with anything?"

I crossed my arms. "You and my kids' safety is my main concern. I will respect your privacy, but I would like to know who you surround yourself with and have in and out."

She rolled her eyes. "When and if I start dating will be my business until I feel the need to share. You won't monitor who I allow in here."

I bit down on my back teeth. On the plus side, she confessed she wasn't seeing anyone which surprisingly put me at ease.

"I trust your judgment."

An amused expression formed on her face. "I'm glad. I guess I'm moving then." She rubbed her belly and looked around the open space again.

Knowing she and my kids would be right downstairs was assuring for me. The fact that I didn't have to force her here like I originally thought it would come down to, made it better. It was good thing that me and Indigo seemed to be on the same page a lot of the time. It made this new relationship between us function better.

Chapter Seventeen

Indigo

Today was the day; my house was packed up and I was awaiting
the movers to come load up the boxes and transfer them to the
condo. I didn't realize how much stuff I truly had until it was time to
move everything.

"It's gonna be weird not having you in Butter Ridge Falls
anymore," Charley commented as we headed for my living room.

I glanced at her. It was like déjà vu from my graduation. My family
waited patiently in my living room. They had come over to finish
helping me pack.

"You act like I'm going far. It's barely an hour away."

"Yeah, but still." She shrugged. "I can't just pop up over here and
bother you when I want." She rolled her eyes and huffed. "Now I gotta
make a drive to see you and my nephews." My stomach knotted. It
hadn't occurred to me at the time that my family wouldn't be right up
the street anymore. Not only my family, but my job was further
away too.

"Aren't you the one who encouraged me to take the condo in the
first place?"

"I mean yeah, I think you're crazy for waiting this long. I'm just
saying it sucks."

We went into my living room where our parents, brother, and Audrey were. "You're welcome over anytime." I bumped her with my shoulder.

Time was winding down and in a couple short months, I would be delivering. My doctor told me at my last appointment that she felt I would only go to eight months and if that was the case, I only had two left.

"Everything in your kitchen is packed and stacked on that wall over there," my mom let me know when I took a seat on the couch. I laid my head on her shoulder and yawned.

"I appreciate you all coming over and helping me." I rubbed my stomach. "I know this was short notice and everything."

Just last week, I was telling Silas I would move into the condo he offered me and here I was now, moving. According to him, he didn't want to waste any time. He had called a cleaning company to come and deep clean the place since it hadn't been touched since he first bought the building and assured me he would handle the moving company. It really shocked me knowing he had paid the rest of my lease as well.

"So, you're really letting this man uproot your whole life?" Myles spoke. When I looked over at him, I saw he was sitting against the wall frowning at me.

"He's not uprooting anything. I chose to do this."

"I'm sure he didn't leave you a choice."

"What's your problem? You act like she's being taken prisoner or something!" Charley spat.

"I'm sorry if I don't like the fact that this random guy got my sister pregnant and is now forcing her to stay with him." I sat up straight.

"No one is forcing me to do anything. Everyone in this room knows I can't be forced to do anything I don't want to do. I'm trying to do what's best for my kids. Being closer to their dad will be good for them. He deserves to involved with them just as much as I am."

"And there's nothing wrong with that!" my mom cut in, her eyes cut in my brother's direction. "Myles, stop it. Your sister can take care of herself. She's doing the right thing."

"We don't even know that guy." He stood up and shoved his hands into his pocket.

"Come take a walk with me." My dad walked over to my brother and wrapped his arm around him. He didn't give him time to object.

I watched as the two headed for my front door.

Sighing, my shoulders fell forward, and I closed my eyes.

"Do think I'm doing the right thing? Is this too drastic?"

Opening my eyes, I turned them to my mom. She was smiling at me with a smile only a mother could give. It was patient, soft, and warm.

"I think it's about time you stop being so strong all the time." She placed her hand on my knee and patted it lightly. "Your whole life, from the moment you could walk, you were independent. You barely crawled as a baby before you started walking. It was then I knew you were gonna be my problem child. You were always mature for your age, stood on your own, and helped with your younger siblings without any fuss. When it came to school you kept good grades, studied hard, and never got in trouble." Her smile grew some.

"I always wanted you to be more of a rebel but you weren't; your sister and your brother gave us hell, but not you. Always had your nose in a book, focusing on some science experiment. As you grew it seemed your independence grew as well. If you could find a solution on your own, you would without asking for help. Even in grad school, me and dad offered to pay it for you since you worked so hard to get there and still you refused. You worked yourself raggedy to be able to pay yourself as well as maintain an A average in classes."

Mom paused and squeezed my knee. I wanted to object what she was saying, but I couldn't. I had a hard time accepting help. It wasn't on purpose, I was just wired like that. It was easier for me to get a job done on my own rather than rely on someone else.

"You're about to have two babies, Indi. One is challenging, but you're having two. My oldest girl never was the one to do anything half-ass." My front door opened, but I kept my eyes on my mom. "You've been handling things on your own for so long, it's okay to let your guard down and finally let someone take care of you. You don't

148

always have to be strong, Indi. I get it, giving someone control is scary for you, but it doesn't mean you're weak if you do it. Silas offering you a bigger place for you and your kids to be comfortable is a good thing. He's doing what he feels is best for you and his kids, and there is nothing wrong with that."

"Don't allow anyone to make you think it's wrong either. Sometimes, stepping back and allowing someone else to take the lead is necessary. I get it, you're still getting to know each other, but how can you fully learn someone if you keep your guard up all the time? If that man who has the resources to help you wants to, let him. Don't fight what's being given to you. In the end, it's best for you and your kids if you and the dad are on the same page."

"Hell you didn't even date, Indigo. You never took time to just let your hair down and enjoy life. You were always in control and the leader. Taking second place is okay at times too."

I processed her words and nibbled on the corner of my bottom lip. What she was saying made sense, but it was still kind of hard. Silas liked to have control, like me, and I wasn't sure how that would work out.

"Your mom's right, Indi." I looked up at my dad. He held his hand out for me and when I grabbed it, he pulled me up to him. "The hardest thing for a father is to let their daughter go and allow another man to take care of them. If I didn't think Silas was a good man, I would have more objections. You're a smart girl, always have been. Out all my kids, I never felt the need to worry about you because you weren't irrational about anything. You thought things through before you did them and it seemed like every decision you made, you always weighed out your options. I'll never steer you wrong, and I'll never let you allow anyone to make you feel guilty for doing what's best for you and your kids. It's okay to let someone put you first and take care of you."

Tears clouded my eyes, and I threw myself into my dad. He pulled me into a tight hug and kissed the top of my head.

"I love you, Daddy."

"I love you too."

My kids stirred in my stomach.

Pulling away, I looked at my mom. "I love you too."

She smiled at me.

"So yeah let rich baby daddy take care of you and don't feel bad about it!" Charley commented.

I groaned and closed my eyes.

"Just don't become one of those girls who get lost in a guy and lose themselves, okay?" When I opened my eyes, my brother was in front of me. He had a stoic look on his face, but it only caused me to grin. I pulled my little brother into me and hugged him as tight as my stomach allowed.

"I love you, knucklehead. Don't worry, I'm still gonna be me."

Myles had always had me growing up. I believe the thought of me having a boyfriend or someone significant in my life made my brother jealous. He never had to share me with anyone else before, but he had to know it wouldn't change anything with us.

"I'm always gonna be your big sister and no one will change that."

He mumbled something I couldn't make out just as someone knocked on my door.

"That's probably rich baby daddy!" Audrey called out.

Pulling away from my brother, I smacked my lips. "Not you too."

She snickered. "It's kind of catchy." She snatched my door open and it was Silas on the other side.

Oddly, my heart stumbled in my chest and blood warmed through my veins.

"Hey!"

Silas stepped inside my house and greeted everyone before laying eyes on me. "You all set?" His eyes wandered around my living room.

I nodded. "Yep. Everything's packed."

He waved his hands. "Good, the movers will take care of every-thing. While they're doing that I want to show you something. Step outside with me."

Curiosity filled me. My brows pulled together and my nose scrunched.

I made my way to him and the moment I got close, he placed a hand on my lower back, and that touch sent a spark up my spine. He did it so often now that I should've expected it, but the way it affected my body was new. The simple gesture always seemed to caress my senses like a silky blanky.

When we got outside, Silas moved away from me and walked over to my driveway. My mouth parted when he stopped near a Range Rover which I noticed wasn't his truck. This one was gold, whereas his was matte black.

"Silas?" I questioned.

"You mentioned how it was getting harder for you to get in and out of cars because of how low they were so I decided to fix the problem. A 2023 Range Rover Autobiography fresh off the lot."

"Wait…"

He opened the door and picked something off the seat. He didn't close the door while he made his way back to me.

"Here. It's yours."

"You…mine? Silas, I can't," I stuttered.

He squinted his eyes. "Of course, you can. You need something higher and when the twins get here it'll give you more room since you'll have two of everything. It's perfect."

My heart danced to an erratic rhythm in my chest. Goosebumps prickled my arms as the hairs on it raised.

"Honey, this is one of the moments we just spoke of. Don't be too proud to accept a gift," my dad's voice sounded behind me.

I glanced at him over my shoulder and his eyes were on Silas'. The two seemed to be having their own conversation silently.

"I don't know what to say."

"Thank you, is typically what people say." A crooked grin spilled on Silas's face.

My eyes went to the truck and then back to him. "I know you hate when I make decisions for you, but this was the easiest solution to your problem. I made sure to get it put in your name too, so you don't have to worry about that."

I pushed out a deep breath and smiled. "Thank you, Silas. I love it." I moved forward and hugged him.

His arms wrapped around me, and I closed my eyes and inhaled him. He always had a clean, fresh scent to him.

"Come through rich baby daddy! C'mon let's go check it out." Charley rushed past us towards the truck, causing me to laugh.

I released Silas and turned to follow behind her. Truly, I would've been a fool to turn down such a nice and luxurious gift.

"Damn, this baby is nice."

I couldn't disagree.

When I mentioned the hassle with cars, I didn't expect Silas to go out and buy me a truck. Normally, him doing this without consulting me would've annoyed me and would've pissed me off regardless of how nice the gift was, but I was learning that was Silas. He had been controlled so much in his life that now he craved to have it and when he saw an issue, he handled it without any thought. It wasn't to be an asshole, it was just how he was, sort of like me. In many ways, I could relate to him.

Looking over my shoulder, I watched him as him and my parents spoke. Audrey had made her way to us, and she and Charley were having fun exploring my new truck while I had to force the giddy feeling down that was forming inside me.

———

My eyes fluttered open and for a second, a slight panic shot through me, unable to remember where I was. Slowly, my mind calmed and I remembered I was in Silas' living room.

After the move today, I ended up eating with him at his place since my place was full of boxes outside of my bigger furniture. Silas had his chef prepare a meal that was waiting for us once everything was finished. My family stayed around for a while, helping me unpack some things and get things in order before heading home.

After we finished eating, I took place on Silas' couch where I found something on Netflix. The day was starting to catch up to me, and all I wanted to do was kick my feet up for a bit. He didn't seem to mind me hanging around and even came and sat by me with his laptop for a while. I wasn't sure when I fell asleep, but now I noticed he had disappeared.

Grabbing my phone from the table next to me, I noticed it was a little past midnight.

Stretching, I blinked a couple times to adjust my eyes and pushed myself off the couch. I was ready to go home to shower and climb in my bed, but I wanted to let Silas know I was leaving.

Slowly, I trekked through the condo until I got to his office where I heard movement and saw light.

Knocking on the door, I pushed it open and peeked inside.

Silas was sitting behind his desk with a glass in his hand, eyes locked on the computer screen.

"I hope you're not working this late," I spoke, causing him to jump.

I snickered, realizing he hadn't even noticed me. "I thought you were still sleep." His brows wiggled. "You okay? You need something?"

My eyes wandered around the office. This was the first time I had been in here since I stopped working for him.

"I'm sorry for falling asleep. I didn't know how tired I was."

He waved me off and his computer dinged. "Damnit!" He grunted, slamming his hand down on the desk. My eyes shot open.

"Is everything okay?"

He looked back at me, this time it was as if he had forgotten I was there that quick. "Yeah, I just lost ten grand though." From the light on his computer and the moonlight peeking in from window, I saw his jaw clenched.

His computer dinged again. "What? What are you doing?"

"Poker," he said stiffly. His eyes went back to the screen.

"You're up past midnight playing poker?" One of my brows raised.

"Losing at poker is more like it. I'm off tonight."

My eyes wandered around the room again. When they landed back on Silas, he had finished off the brown liquid in his glass.

"Is this normal for you?"

"I have insomnia bad, so I might as well make money if I can't sleep. Well normally, I make money. Fuck it, double or nothing."

My eyes enlarged. "You're about to bet twenty thousand dollars?"

"Gotta spend money to make it." When his focus turned back to me, he was grinning.

I scanned his face over, taking in his profile against the moonlight. His classically handsome feature on full display. Everything about Silas screamed self-confidence.

"Wow, well good luck with that." I licked my lips. "I was just coming in here to tell you I was gonna head downstairs."

His mouth pressed together. He tapped his mouse a few times before standing up.

"I'll walk you down."

Quickly, I shook my head. "You don't have to. It's just one floor lower."

His brows pulled together. "And I'm not letting you leave alone regardless of how secure this place is. You're pregnant with my kids, I might add. I'm walking you."

I didn't fight him any further. You had to have a code to get in the parking garage and if you used the guest entrance, you still needed to be buzzed up if you didn't have the elevator code. Silas had a security system installed for me, although I didn't think I needed it. Knowing all that, he still felt the need to walk me to my place. It made a fire ignite inside me, and the gesture struck a vibrant chord inside me.

Nothing else was said between us. Silas guided me to the front of his condo, and we headed for the elevator once we were in the hall.

When the elevator dinged, Silas' hand moved to my lower back causing my pulse to skitter alarmingly.

I peeked at him out the corner of my eye, and he had a neutral expression on his face. It was easy to admit something about Silas brought me comfort. I just had to make sure I didn't start blurring lines between us.

Chapter Eighteen

Silas

Since the night Indigo moved in and came up to eat with me, we'd made it an unspoken rule between the two of us. If I wasn't working late, I made sure enough food was made for the both of us. I still paid to have meals prepped for her throughout the week, but it felt nice having dinner with her a couple times as well.

"I want to show you something," I told her after finishing the last of the stuffed chicken we were eating. My chef made stuffed chicken, garlic mash potatoes, and roasted broccoli for us.

She glanced at me under her lashes and pushed her locs out her face. "Is everything okay?"

Bobbing my head, I pushed myself from the table and stood up. "Everything's fine." Making my way to her, I held my hand out to help her up.

She didn't ask any more questions as we headed to the back of my condo near the bedrooms. "Fiona found some interior designers that came out earlier in the week." I stopped in front of one of my bedroom doors and pushed it open.

"Silas. Wow, this room is gorgeous!" Her eyes lit up as she slipped into the nursey. I decided to keep the rooms simple and had them decorated in colors, rather than theme. This one being royal blue and gold.

"The other room, matches this one except I did forest green and gold in that one." She made her way around the room, running her hands along the crib.

"This is the one?" She whipped around. I smirked.

"The one you got from the store. I remembered you said it was a good one so I ordered it too." I shrugged.

Indigo tugged on her bottom lip. I was surprised to see tears fill her eyes. "Wait? Why are you tearing up?" Panic shot through me.

She shook her head and used the back of her hand to wipe her eyes. "It's not what you think."

Rushing towards her, I grabbed her waist and ran my eyes over. "Are you in pain? Do you need to go to the hospital?"

"No. I'm fine." Her tears ran down her face. Her words rushed.

My heart clenched in my chest and throat grew tight. "Indigo. Why?" My words were shushed by her lips on mine. She grabbed my face and yanked it down, crashing her mouth into mine.

I was caught off guard by her actions. Her tongue found its way inside my mouth and instantly, I took possession of the kiss, owning her mouth as my mouth, sucking on her tongue.

My fingers dug into her side and her stomach pressed against mine. Blood raged through my veins down to my groin.

It wasn't until Indigo pulled away, breathing heavily that I felt some control coming over me.

"I'm sorry," she whispered, shifting her eyes. Her lips swollen with gloss smeared on them. "I just…seeing this. Knowing you're really on board with being a father now, it made me emotional. Blame it on the babies." She giggled nervously.

Reaching a hand up, I wiped some lip gloss from under her bottom lip. "I told you I came to accept things a long time ago. I'm in this. *We're* in this."

Her bottom lip trembled. "I've been told I have an issue with letting go and allowing someone else to take the lead. I want to trust that you'll always have our kids' best interest at heart."

"Not just them, but you as well," I let her know. "I come off as a control freak I know that, but I want you to know I don't do it because I want to actually control you it's just that—"

Her eyes softened. "I know. I get it. I don't take offense to it anymore."

"I just want you to know that when it comes to the twins, we're on the same page. They'll be here before we know it, and I don't want you to think I'm not prepared."

"I never thought you weren't, but this does assure me."

"C'mon, I want to show you the other room."

I didn't know the first thing about what all I needed to buy when it came to babies, so I told Fiona to go to the store and do as she pleased. She had nieces and nephews and seemed to know what to get. Because of her, both babies' rooms were loaded and prepared for their arrival.

"I know we just moved you in the condo, but do you think you'll want a house?" I asked randomly.

Indigo was looking through the baby clothes in the closet and took a second to glance at me. "Eventually, yeah. Once the twins are up and moving, I want them to have a yard to play in." She paused and eyes narrowed. "I don't need you buying me a house, though."

I hummed and shoved my hands in my pockets while she continued looking through the clothes.

I wasn't going to entertain what just said. When the time came for her to move, I would make sure her and my kids had nothing but the best.

———

"Don't forget the annual charity ball is next week," Fiona let me know.

My head instantly began to throb at the thought. I had no issue giving to charity, but I loathed these events. All it was, was a bunch of people competing on who had the most money and could donate the most.

"Shit, it's that time again, huh?" I leaned back in my desk chair.

Today, I was working from home and planned on it being a short day. In a couple hours, I was meeting Indigo at the clinic she worked at. She had mentioned wanting to do some genetic testing to learn about my family's health history or something like that for the twins.

"Can't I just write a check and call it a day? I'm not tryna be around all them fake ass people."

"Now you know that wouldn't look good on your part. You must make an appearance." Sighing, I knew she was right. Even if it was for only an hour, I had to show face.

"Why don't you ask Indigo to go with you?" Fiona suggested after a couple minutes of silence.

"Indigo? Why would I do that?" A sly look appeared on her face.

"The two of you have gotten cozy with each other, right? Maybe having her there will make it more bearable for you."

I rubbed my small beard and thought it over. "I doubt she'll even want to go."

"You won't know if you don't ask." Bringing my eyes to meet Fiona's, I gave her a curious glance.

"Why do you sound like that?"

"Like what?" She batted her lashes.

"Like you got something up your sleeve?"

Fiona shook her head. "I don't know what you're talking about. I just notice you and Indigo spending more time together. You don't get tense when she's brought up anymore. I even notice you smiling when she's brought up now."

My tongue dragged across my top teeth. "You're reading into things too much."

"Or maybe I'm reading into things enough. When you first found out about her pregnancy, all communication went through me. Now you talk to her directly and spend time with her. I think you're starting to like her." Her sly grin grew.

My face stayed blank as I neither confirmed nor denied her statement. If I was being honest, I wasn't sure how I felt about Indigo anymore. I enjoyed being around her and the more I learned about her the more I appreciated she was the one who I impregnated.

"You can go ahead and leave. I'm gonna finish up here then head out," I let her know.

She clicked her tongue and her tapping on her iPad sounded. "I'll make sure to include you'll have a plus one."

Again, I was silent.

Fiona left my home office, and I was left alone to my thoughts. I set my work to the side, folded my hands, and placed my elbows on the desk in deep thought. For so long I fought the thought of being in a relationship, and I wasn't even sure I was ready to take that step. What I did know was that whatever was forming between me and Indigo didn't bother me, and I was interested to see just how far it would go.

———

When I pulled up to the clinic Indigo worked at, I threw my car in park and turned it off, about to climb out when something caught my eye, causing me to pause.

My eyes narrowed as I watched Indigo smiling in some older guy's face. He was grinning down at her, and when his hand landed on her shoulder, my muscles taut and jaw clenched.

The guy said something that made Indigo laugh and bob her head. As I stared at the duo, I realized I had seen the guy before. It was the same guy in the photos my mom had shown me.

An inkling feeling that I'd never experienced before filled my stomach. In reality, I knew I had no reason to feel some type away about Indigo smiling in another man's face, but knowing she was carrying my kids made all that reasoning disappear.

Snatching my door open, I slammed it shut and stalked over to the front of the clinic.

"Indigo," I called out once I was close enough.

Both their eyes snapped in my direction. She looked shocked at first but then smiled.

"Silas. Hi. Is it time for our meet-up, already?" I approached her and stood at her side, sizing up the guy in front of us.

"Who is this?"

"Oh, right, this is your first time here. This is my boss, Dr. Foe. He runs the lab here at the clinic. Dr. Foe, this is Silas, my kid's dad."

The guy held his hand out. "Nice to meet you."

My eyes dropped to it then back up to him. "Likewise." I grabbed his hand, giving it a firm shake. He stared at me confused.

Releasing his hand, I turned to face Indigo. "I'm here. Should we get to it?"

Nodding her head, she spoke to Dr. Foe first. "I'll see you tomorrow. Thank you again for the help."

His smile returned. "No problem. I'll see you tomorrow."

A frown returned on my face. I wasn't feeling the stars I saw in Indigo's orbs as she watched the doctor.

I cleared my throat. "I don't have all day."

Her attention left the doctor and cheeks flushed. "Oh right. Sorry. C'mon."

We headed into the building and down a hallway. "So what are we doing here, again?" I questioned, observing the rooms as we passed them.

Indigo explained what she planned to do today, and I nodded. "And you think something could be wrong with the babies?."

She shook her head. "No, I'm not saying that. I was just curious. I don't know a lot about you and you don't talk to your family so this was the only way to learn. In here." She nodded to a room.

"I'll get you set up."

Turning around, I surprised Indigo when I grabbed her waist. Her eyes widened. My hands moved to her stomach and I cuffed it, running my thumbs across it.

"Have they been active today?"

A small, toothless grin formed on her face. "They're always active. Right now they're sleep though."

Her stomach was hard and more of an oval shape than a circle. "And you are feeling okay?"

She pressed her lips together and nodded.

I grinned. "Good." I released her stomach and looked around the room. "Let's get started."

Chapter Nineteen

Indigo

"Fiona, I don't know about this," I whined while eating my fruit salad.

She took a seat next to me and smiled softly. "Don't worry about it, Indigo, I'll handle everything."

I pulled on my bottom lip with my teeth. "So you want me to get dressed up and go to this party when I look like a blimp?" My mouth turned upside down.

"Girl, you're beautiful stop it. I know it might be unconventional, but the event isn't all that bad. Plus, Silas wants you there with him."

Squinting my eyes, I side-eyed her. "He does?" One of my eyebrows lifted.

"Yeah, girl." She snickered. "You've been growing on Boss Man, believe it or not." Her words sent a warm feeling through my stomach and up to my chest.

"That's good to hear, I guess. Hopefully, it last."

Fiona tucked her lips into her mouth and tapped her fingers on her knee. "Look, I probably shouldn't be telling you this, but listen. I've been working for Silas for years, and in those amount of years he's never focused on solely one woman, which I'm sure you're aware of. But since you've been around, he hasn't had a bunch of women in and out his bed nor has he been so uptight. You know a lot of people misjudge Silas because he uses humor to cover up how he feels a lot, but his parents really did mess him up. He's honestly not a bad guy, and I think you being a part of his life helped him loosen up and let his guard down."

I shoved some fruit salad in my mouth. "Way to make a girl blush."

"Be honest with me, Indigo. How do you feel about Silas? I know your start was rocky, but what about now?"

She tilted her head to the side with a smirk on her face.

My cheeks heated more. "We've formed a good friendship over the past few months."

"Just a friendship?"

"I mean I might not have a lot of dating experience, but I know not to put myself out there for a guy whose made it known he doesn't want to date or anything serious." It would be easy to admit I wanted to take things further with Silas, but if he didn't want the same there was no sense of setting myself up for failure.

"I promise you, Indigo, it isn't like that. Silas likes you, trust me, I've been around long enough to know."

Piercing my lips together, I turned my body so I was fully facing her. "Why are you pushing this?"

"There's no certain reason why other than I don't want Silas to grow old and lonely. I think you're good for him, you and the twins." Her eyes dropped down.

The warm feeling inside me grew hotter. My heart thumped wildly in my chest.

"Okay. I guess I can go to the ball then."

Her smile grew. "Great. I'll take care of everything else."

———

I pulled my locs into a bun on top of my head before moving over to my shower and turning it on. I had Jhene Aiko's latest album playing through my Bluetooth stereo.

"*I been alone all night. I got you on my mind,*" I sang along and moved back to the sink so I could run through my face routine.

After rinsing my face and opening my eyes, a scream left my mouth and my bladder failed me as I stared at Silas behind me.

"What the fuck!" I shouted, grabbing my chest and whipping around.

His eyes dropped down to the small puddle that formed between my legs then lifted back up at me.

"Silas, what are you doing here! You weren't supposed to use your key to come and go whenever you want!" I tightened my robe.

"I knocked on the door, but when you didn't answer I got worried."

"I couldn't hear because the music and the shower." Reaching over, I grabbed my face towel to dry my face. "What are you doing here?"

He licked his lips, and the way he ran his eyes down my body sent a shock down to my toes. A faint light twinkled in the depths of his hooded orbs.

"Fiona told me you agreed to go to the ball with me."

"Yeah, I did."

"Good, good." His ran his hand over his mouth. He was still eating me up with his eyes. A knot raised in my throat.

When he licked his lips, my eyes locked on them. Between my legs pulsated. My pulse beat in my throat.

"I uh, I was about to get in the shower," I let him know.

Dropping my eyes down, I eyed the noticeable bulge in his slacks. My teeth sunk into the fat of my bottom lip.

"I guess you need some privacy."

Instead of verbally answering, I bobbed my head.

It felt like air in the bathroom electrified. "I'll wait in your room then."

Silas stepped out the bathroom and the moment he was gone, I quickly cleaned up the puddle on the floor, stripped out my robe, and stepped into the shower.

The hot water on my skin felt like heaven to my aching muscles; my back was sore and tight.

Grabbing my loofah and body wash, I squirted some on and began washing my body. With my eyes closed, I envisioned Silas and the way he ate me up with his eyes. Running my loofah over my belly, I brushed it over my mound and a shiver shot through my bottom lips.

It had been so long since I been touched. I had set the boundaries with me and Silas, but the fact he hadn't even tried to convince me otherwise was unsettling. My sex drive had been up and down the further I'd gotten in my pregnancy.

Squeezing my loofah, I released a small moan and ran my hand across the suds over my nipples.

I thought about what Fiona told me earlier. Maybe things with Silas *had* changed and I could make some changes myself.

"Close mouths don't get fed," I muttered and pulled opened the glass door.

"Silas!" I called out. "Silas!"

My blood hummed through my veins as I felt a ripple of excitement shoot through me as Silas stepped inside the bathroom.

"What's wrong!" His words rushed and eyes full of worry bouncing around my bathroom before landing on me.

I snickered seeing how panicked he looked. "I need help cleaning my back, please." His eyes seem to grow darker and mouth parted.

He had laser vision on my body as I pulled the door open more. "Can you come in and help me?" I batted my lashes.

I wasn't good at this and I felt somewhat awkward, but I was horny and wanted my baby daddy at the moment.

Silas loosened his tie before untucking his dress shirt. My insides jangled with excitement as my body ached for his touch. He undid his slacks and pushed them down along with his boxers.

"You sure about this?" he questioned, undoing his shirt.

"I am." A shy smile split my face.

Silas's hand went to his length, and he stroked it slowly, making his way towards me. The water prickled my skin and the moment he stepped inside the shower, my heart lurched in my chest.

Just as I was about to speak, Silas grabbed the back of my neck and pulled me into him. His mouth crashed into mine, instantly dominating it. His tongue sent shivers of desire racing through me.

His length pressed against my stomach and hand went to the small of my back. My head swirled as his kiss grew more possessive. Spirals of ecstasy shot through me.

Silas released me and stared me in the eyes with a smothering flame.

A yelp escaped my mouth when he lifted me up and moved backwards until my back was against the wall.

"This okay with the babies?" His voice low and laced with concern.

"They're fine," I breathlessly replied.

My mouth parted as he lowered me down on his shaft and my head fell back. My fingers dug into his shoulders and my legs tightened around his waist.

Moans fell from my mouth as he started moving in and out of me. Passion inched through my veins. My body vibrated and a shudder shot through me.

Silas' mouth met mine again with a slow, drugging kiss.

"Oh fuck!" I cried when he thrusted deep inside me. My body shook and my nails dug deeper.

"I don't know how much longer Ima last," he murmured against my mouth. His strokes grew sped up, tap dancing against my spot over and over.

"I'm not." My words got caught in my throat.

My stomach tightened as my kids balled up.

As another tingle shot through my body, the floodgates between my legs opened. "Kiss me," I begged him.

Complying with my wishes, our mouths met like metal to a magnetic. Our tongues danced together.

My walls tightened around his dick as it jerked inside me.

My heart thundered.

Lowering my head to Silas' shoulder, I panted lowly with my eyes closed, attempting to catch my breath.

I didn't know how much I needed this until this moment.

Thankfully, the condo had a good water heater and was still hot. Steam filled around us.

Silas slowly lowered me down to the floor. My knees buckled, and he gripped me tighter.

"You good?"

My eyes cut to him and a cocky grin was on his face.

"I'm fine."

The moment I turned to grab my loofah again, Silas' chest pressed against my back. He wrapped his arm around my waist and pulled me into him.

Silas lowered his mouth to my ear. "I got another round in me, once we get out."

My eyes fluttered and head went back against his chest. His warm breath tickled my ear.

This was the first time Silas had ever been this affectionate towards me and it felt nice. I was starting to enjoy these moments between us. My hopes were that they would last and even push further.

Chapter Twenty

Silas

The moment Indigo opened her door, I took her beauty in. The burgundy double layer ruffle dress she had on showed off her growing bump perfectly. The color also looked good against her glowing skin. Even though she was exhausted a lot of the time now, looking at her at this moment you wouldn't know it.

She had gotten her locs retwisted, washed, and done into a twisted updo style that showed her fuller face perfectly. She didn't have any makeup on, outside of the lipstick that matched her dress.

"Damn," I murmured, hungrily eating her up.

"Does the dress look okay?" Her hand ran over the front of her. "Charley and Audrey told me I didn't look huge, but I'm not sure. I feel like a blimp." Again, her hand ran down her stomach. One corner of my mouth lifted in a mirth expression. This was the first time I saw Indigo unsure of herself and it was new for me. She was always sure of herself, but I could tell the closer she got to the end of her pregnancy the more uncomfortable in her skin she grew.

I stepped forward and grabbed her hip, pulling her into me. "You look beautiful. This dress..." I cocked my head back and scanned her over again. "This dress looks great on you too. You have nothing to worry about."

Dipping my head, I kissed the top of her head. "You mean it?"

She batted her lashes and tilted her head up. Pecking her lips lightly, I nodded. "I do. Everyone's gon' see how fine you are the moment you walk inside and not be able to take their eyes off you."

The corners of her mouth lifted. "I hate feeling like this. It's all new to me." The smile in her eyes contained a sensuous flame.

Things with the two of us shifted and there was no denying it. Part of me wanted to push her away, but the other part was feeling the connection between us.

Even when it came to the condo, I was learning to respect her boundaries. After we slept together, Indigo made sure to enforce the fact that I couldn't just use my keys whenever I wanted, and although I told her I was worried because she didn't answer the door, she wasn't tryna hear that. She made sure to let me know by her taking the condo meant having her privacy and boundaries.

My hand rested on the small of her back, and I massaged it lightly. "It's almost over."

She sighed. "I know."

I kissed the top of her head one last time before releasing her. "If you're ready we should go. The car's downstairs."

"Okay, let me grab my purse."

Indigo spun around and went back into her house.

I went into my pocket to check the time. Fiona had texted me about my estimated time of arrival. I responded back quickly and shoved it back into my slacks.

Indigo walked back out, turned, and locked her door.

"Ready!" She grinned at me.

My hand went to the small of her back and we started for the elevator. I didn't care to go to this event, but I believed having Indigo by my side would make it a little more bearable.

———

"Wow, I don't think I've ever been to a more classier looking event," Indigo gushed as we stepped into the event room at the Velez Inn hotel.

"Yeah, these people always go all out."

"I love the Velez Inn. It's such a nice hotel, they chose a great location."

Soft music was playing in the room. People were scattered around talking among themselves.

"We only have to be here an hour tops and then we can leave," I let her know as we headed to the tables to find ours. "Before we take our seats, do you want to go get a plate first?"

She looked up at me with a bright face. "You're asking me, who's carrying two humans inside me, if I'm hungry?" She wagged her brows.

Chuckling, I changed our direction over to where the food was. One thing I can say about these events is they never half-stepped when it came to food.

"What's the event raising money for again?" Indigo questioned as we waited in line.

"St. Jude's Children Hospital."

I grabbed two plates, handing her one. "Thank you. You know I love events like this. It always makes me happy knowing my job is related to these causes."

"That's right, you do research for things like this. How's that going?"

Looking over her shoulder at me, she grinned. "Great, actually! Well kind of. We were able to detect some mutated genes in a kid's sample we were sent that could cause them to have some disabilities. The parents have time to prepare because it was found early. I feel for the parents, but hopefully, they'll handle the news okay." We moved down the buffet line.

"Oh my gosh, everything looks so good!" Indigo was practically watering at the mouth.

We got our food and was heading to our table when the hairs on the back of my neck raised and body tensed as my mom stomped towards us. She had a tight smile on her face, but her eyes were glaring at us.

"Silas Theodore Newton," she gritted through clenched teeth.

"Your middle name is Theodore?" Indigo glanced up at me in amusement.

Ignoring her, I glanced back at my mom. "Hello, Mother. Nice to see you. If you'll excuse us." My hand went to the small of her back, and I went to step around my mom but she halted us.

"How dare you embarrass me by bringing this woman here with all my friends to see." She gave Indigo a disgusted look.

A small snicker escaped Indigo's mouth next to me. "You know if I wasn't seven and a half months pregnant and starving right now, I would stand here and go back and forth with you, but I'm hungry and even your miserable ass won't stand between me and this food. Silas, handle your mama and come find me." She gave my mom a taunting look and grabbed my plate before waddling away.

The way she handled things caused my dick to stir in my slacks. This was the Indigo I was used to, not the one who greeted me at her door earlier. I couldn't keep my attention off her ass either. The twins had filled her behind out nicely.

Mom cleared her throat. Pushing a deep breath out, I turned my attention back to her. I straightened my tie. "Mother, is there something I can help you with?"

She turned and waved to one of her friends with a fake smile. "Why would you bring that girl here, Silas? This is not the environment for her; plus, Spencer is here with her parents. Even though you threw a tantrum the last time you two were around each other, I'm sure it could be overlooked and—"

"If I didn't make it clear the last couple times, I *do not* want Spencer. I'm happy with Indigo and she's having my children. I don't know what it'll take for you to realize you can't control my life and dictate who's in it. Now if you'll excuse me."

"Silas." She sneered. "Our name is respected. I will not allow you to have some nameless woman come in and ruin it! Spencer is a respectable woman, who comes from our world, and she has class, and will look good with you. If you just go with my plans and take the kids from that hussy then we'll be good. Spencer and you can raise them together and they'll grow up with an acceptable life."

My hand ran down my face. I didn't know what it was going to take for my mom to give it up.

My dad had approached her. "There are some people I want you to meet, Honey." He looked at me. "Son." He nodded.

"Dad, please get your wife and explain to her to stay out my life. I'm a grown man who doesn't need her making decisions for me and if she wants to control someone then maybe the two of you need to have another kid. Now if you both excuse me." I stepped around then, leaving my mom standing there as if I'd smacked her.

Rolling my shoulders, I mentally counted to ten. I was stopped by a couple people by the time I made it to the table where Indigo was waiting for me, already eating.

"I hope things went well." Indigo didn't even stop eating while she spoke.

"This is the last place my mom will make a scene at. For now, we're good."

This time, Indigo put her food down and grabbed her napkin, wiping her mouth then turned to face me. "Is this what I must look forward to? Your mom constantly attacking me every time she sees me? Downing me like I'm less than her?" Her face was blank as she stared at me.

Lifting my shoulders and allowing them to fall, I closed my eyes and released a frustrated breath. "I'm doing all I can to get her to stop. Unfortunately, once Pamela Newton puts her mind to something she doesn't let up. I've told you that."

"So what you're saying is I just have to deal with it?"

My eyes squinted. "No. I'm not saying that. What I'm saying is don't let my mom get to you. Ima do whatever I need to do to keep her away from you. I don't want you worrying about her, a'right."

My hand went to the back of the chair. "Yo mama better be worried. I'm not gon' be pregnant too much longer and it's only so much disrespect I'll keep accepting. Don't let the brainy girl fool you." She pouted her lips out.

Chuckling, I licked my lips. "You threatening my mom?"

"I mean…" She smirked.

I shook my head. "I hear you, boss."

I turned to my plate.

The evening went on and the host of tonight's event made sure to make an announcement greeting and thanking everyone for attending. Thankfully, my mom had stayed out our way. That didn't mean I didn't miss the glares from her.

Indigo had made a good distraction for the night. I was able to introduce her to a couple people I associated with and thankfully, no one treated her like she was beneath them.

Once I noticed the evening starting to catch up with Indigo, it was time to call it a night. I had made my donation and stayed long enough.

"I 'preciate you coming out with me tonight. I know this might not be your crowd. Honestly, it isn't mine either," I leaned down and whispered in Indigo's ear before pressing my lips against it. She leaned into me and a soft sigh fell from her mouth.

"It wasn't bad."

"Yeah a'right. We can leave now though. I see all on your face how tired you are."

"Are you sure?" She yawned. "I don't want to pull you away if you're really not ready."

"I been here an hour longer than I wanted. Trust me we can go. I said my goodbyes already too."

"Okay." She smiled lightly.

Standing up, I helped her up and guided her towards the exit.

"Silas!" a feminine voice sounded just as we were at the exit. Stopping for a moment, I glanced over and inwardly groaned as Ria made her way towards me. Of course, she was dressed to the nines with diamonds dripping off her.

I cleared my throat. "Ria," I acknowledged, keeping my voice bland.

For a moment, my eyes dipped down to her overly enhanced cleavage that was barely being contained in the dress she was wearing then snapped back up to her face.

"It's been a while since I've seen you." She seductively batted her lashes with a sly grin on her face. I noticed her words slightly slurred. Typically, she was more discreet than this.

"Yeah and it's a reason to that." I pulled Indigo. "This is Indigo. Indigo, Ria."

"Nice to meet you." Indigo smiled.

Ria's smile dropped, and she glanced at Indigo before chuckling then turned back to me. "I guess that's why you haven't responded back to me." She nodded towards Indigo's bulging stomach and flipped her hair over her shoulders.

My hold on Indigo tightened. "Yes, it is. Indigo is expecting as you can see, so my time has been occupied."

"There you are, baby, I was looking for you." Ria's husband, Deacon, walked up on her and wrapped his arm around Ria, pressing his lips against her temple.

His eyes fell on me. "Ah, Silas it's nice to see you again." He held his hand out.

"Deacon." I shook his hand.

"Excuse Ria. Baby, come with me please. I have some people I want you to meet." She gave him a tight smile.

"Sure, babe. Silas, it was nice seeing you again."

Chapter Twenty-One

Indigo

T he evening went surprisingly well outside of Silas's mom
confronting us and the weird exchange when we were leaving.
Silas hardly left my side tonight, and I was even surprised when he
started introducing me to people.

Currently, we were on our way back home. My eyes were heavy,
but I felt relaxed. It had been a while since I went to a social event and
enjoyed myself. Even the twins were hyped up while we were there.

I had my seat leaned back, enjoying whatever Silas had playing
from his phone. Turning my head, I stared at his side profile for a
moment. His small, groomed beard was glistening from whatever he
used to keep it clean. There was an inherent strength in his face. There
was no denial my baby daddy was devastatingly handsome. My
stomach fluttered; even while he was driving he had a commanding
manner.

"So…" I started, tracing my eyes down his body and back up to his
face. "I'm assuming you and that girl are involved?" The moment the
girl approached us, I peeped her demeanor and how she tried sizing me
up. Her top lip curled up the moment her irises landed on my stomach.

Silas wet his lips, but his body stayed laxed. "You're referring to
Ria, I assume?" His eyes stayed focused on the road.

"That's the only woman who approached us like she had an issue." My head tilted back and a small smirk formed on my face. Honestly, a bit of jealousy shot through when I realized what was going on. Ria's body language read that she had some kind of relationship with Silas. The fact that she was married was shocking, however.

A small hint of mirth ticked on Silas' mouth, and this time he glanced over at me. "Currently, there is nothing going on with us."

"But there was?"

His head bobbed. "While she was married?"

Again, he nodded. "Ria and I used to deal with one another, but I haven't had any dealings with her in months."

I tugged on my bottom lip, ignoring the small ache that passed through my chest. "And I'm assuming her husband didn't know?"

He shrugged. "I didn't know she was married the first time I met up with her, but the way she makes it seem, they have some kind of open relationship."

He glanced at me again. "Does that bother you?"

My face dropped. "Why would it bother me?"

"I don't know, meeting a woman I've had relations with might make you uncomfortable."

"If the roles were reversed would you be uncomfortable?"

"Considering I'm the *only* man who *has had* relations with you, that doesn't matter."

I rolled my eyes and shifted in my seat. "Okay true. But when you came to my job you were upset about Dr. Foe, right?"

His jaw tensed visibly which made me grin. "You were, right? You were jealous?"

I didn't bring it up before because it was honestly kind of refreshing to me and made me feel good inside. Silas was so anti being a couple, but it was clear that he felt some type of way about Dr. Foe.

A small, deep chuckle fell from his lips. "Baby, can't no one on this earth make me jealous, but a'right. I'll admit I wasn't feeling how you was grinning in that nigga's face."

Warmth filed through my chest as my heart thumped wildly.

"So the Ria girl? You said you aren't dealing with her anymore?"

"Nah."

"Why not? Since when?"

He pulled up to the parking garage gate and entered the code to lift it. Silas didn't answer my question right away. Instead, he parked his truck and then turned his body to face me. He observed me for a moment as if he was looking for something. Whatever it was he must have found because the crooked half-grin split his face.

"I haven't touched that woman since I came to terms with you having my kids. I haven't touched any woman if we're being honest."

The pounding in my chest raised to my ears. I swallowed the lump that had formed in my throat.

"Why?" This time my voice was low and I sat up straighter.

Silas' eyes were sharp and assessing. Again, he searched my face as if he was trying to reach into my thoughts.

Suddenly, his orbs darkened with emotions.

"I can't tell you, to be honest. I just haven't had the urge and my attention's kind of been occupied."

My breathing faltered and blood rushed through my veins.

"Nothing wrong with that."

Silas reached over and brushed my jaw lightly with his fingertips. "I'm going out of town in a couple days for an event. I want you to come along with me."

His request shocked me. I was still fuzzy when it came to me and Silas. He wasn't as uptight with me anymore. We spent a lot more time together, but he hadn't made any indication that his feelings for me had changed.

"An event?"

He nodded, stroking my chin. The hairs on the back of my neck raised and heated. "The derby is coming up and I'll be attending. I want you to join me." His eyes dropped down to my stomach. "As long as you feel up to it."

It made me feel good knowing that Silas wanted to willingly spend more time with me. When I first found out I was pregnant, I felt like a burden he was forced to deal with because I was carrying his kids. Now it didn't feel like that. His interest in me felt genuine.

"I have work."

"It'll be on the weekend, so you won't have to worry. I've already booked the room, and I have a suite at the track. All you must do is agree."

Knowing that this would more than likely be the last time I'd be able to do something like this until after the babies, I decided to agree. Not to mention, I enjoyed hanging out with Silas.

"Okay. Sure." I grinned while my heart fluttered.

Finally, the two of us exited the car and headed to the elevator so we could head to our separate houses.

When we got to my floor, a small wave a sadness shot through me. I wasn't ready to leave Silas, but I wasn't sure if I should voice it or not.

Silas placed his hands on the small of my back and guided me off the elevator. He led me to my door and I took my time grabbing my keys.

Silas stared at me curiously when he noticed I made no motion to open my door.

"What's wrong?" His brows furrowed.

I nibbled on my bottom lip while my running my hand over my stomach.

"I don't wanna be alone tonight," I confessed, gazing up at him. I batted my lashes as my heart ticked loudly. It was a forward gesture, and I wasn't sure if Silas would be on board.

Silas wrapped his arm around my waist and it caught me off guard when he pulled me closer to me. My stomach pressed against his stomach. He dipped his head and pressed his lips against my forehead.

"I was going to recommend you stay the night with me, but I didn't want to seem controlling."

Silas still had his ways, but he was doing better with not being overcontrolling and forcing his way.

A small giggle left my mouth and I leaned up, pressing my lips against his. My chest arched into him.

"C'mon. Let's go upstairs." He nipped my bottom lip and pulled back.

I nodded.

I knew the two of us would have to have a conversation about our status. We had agreed to co-parent, but this felt more than that. Something shifted with us. I wasn't sure when or why, but I couldn't even say I was upset about it.

——

"Look who's all smiles today," my mom commented, sitting next to me.

Taking a drink of my lemonade, I tried to hide my smile behind my glass.

"I don't know what you're talking about."

Her head turned to my dad. "Are you seeing this?"

He nodded with a smirk. "I am, and I can only guess where the smile is coming from."

Playfully, I rolled my eyes. "You guys are exaggerating. I'm just in a good mood. I had a good day at work today and now I'm coming to see my parents."

"Keep telling yourself that, honey." My mom snickered. "I'm actually glad you're here. I wanted to get your thoughts on a baby shower."

"Baby shower?" Surprisingly, I hadn't even thought of a shower. I had pretty much everything I needed for the twins, for the most part.

She nodded. "Yes, you haven't mentioned one, but it's only right we throw you one. This is your first pregnancy.

"Oh…I mean I really haven't thought about it. It's not really needed." I scratched my chin. "Do we have to?"

Mom frowned. "Well, of course we do! What new mom doesn't want a baby shower?"

"I'm just ready to meet my kids. I don't care about all that stuff. Do what you want. It doesn't matter to me." I shrugged and drank more of my lemonade.

My mom didn't seem very happy with my response, but it was the truth. The only thing I was preparing for was a healthy delivery. Time was growing closer, and mentally, I was preparing the fact I would have to care for two humans outside of me.

"How are things with you and Silas?" my dad interjected.

The smile returned to my face. "Good. We've grown closer over the past couple weeks."

"Are you two a couple now?" my mom asked.

"I didn't say all that, but I don't know, we're good still."

"Just don't accept less than what you deserve." The look on my dad's face became serious.

Leaning forward, I couldn't have been happier to have the kind of parents I did. "I know, Daddy, don't worry. Silas knows what I expect and won't accept."

"Is his family excited about the twins? You don't mention them," my mom questioned.

That made my smile dim. Just the thought of Silas' parents caused me to roll my eyes.

"He's not close with his family and his parents... his mom doesn't exactly approve."

"Approve of what, exactly?" My mom's mouth turned upside down.

I shrugged. "That I'm good enough to have her grandkids. She believes money should deal with money." I waved my hand. "It's all nonsense really."

"And who the hell does she think she is, telling my baby she isn't good enough! Who is this woman, I would love to have a conversation with her!" My mom's head cocked back and her voice heightened.

I snickered. "Mom, relax. I don't care what she thinks. She's upset because she wants Silas with one of her friend's daughters and he's against it. I'm not worried about that lady."

"And what does Silas have to say about all this?" my dad inquired.

My smile returned. "He's actually on my side. He doesn't agree with his mom and makes sure to check her every time she voices how she feels."

"He better. I'm not gonna allow anyone to make you feel less than you are! Any man would be lucky to have a child with you! Regardless

179

of how much money they have! My daughter is a catch!" My mom was practically steaming out the ears which was slightly comical to me.

"I know that, Mommy. That's why I'm not bothered. I know what I bring to the table. Hell I got my master's in chemistry and chemical engineering. If that doesn't scream worthy, I don't know what does. We may not be as wealthy as them, but we have money too. Humph."

"It sure does! My baby has beauty and brains!"

A few moments later, my brother came waltzing into the room.

"How come I feel like I've barely seen you since you've been home?" I stood up so I could hug him. I knew he was due to go back to school soon and it felt like we'd rarely spent any time together.

"Because everything else has been occupying your time. Why does it look like you get bigger and bigger every time I see you?"

Frowning, I rolled my eyes. "Thanks a lot."

"Son, word of advice, never tell a woman that. Pregnant or not." My dad chuckled, shaking his head.

"I'm just saying!" Myles eyed my belly before taking a seat next to me.

"Considering I'm carrying two kids, it's a given my stomach grows more than normal."

"I'm just glad you're having boys. I get tired being the only one."

"If I'm being honest, I am too." I rubbed my stomach just as one of my sons kicked.

"Have you thought of names yet?" my dad asked.

I shook my head. "I guess that's something that needs to be considered soon." Out of all the things to be considered, I hadn't even thought about names for my sons. Silas hadn't mentioned them either.

"I think they should be named after me. At least one of them." My brother beamed. I gave Myles a blank stare.

"Yeah, I'll get right on that."

I stayed at my parents' house a little long before preparing to leave, not before my mom made me a to-go plate of the food she cooked for the day. Both my sons had been extra active today, draining my energy, and I was ready to relax in the comfort of my bed.

Chapter Twenty-Two

Silas

"Wow," Indigo gushed around the hotel suite as I closed the door behind us.

It was the weekend of the derby and we had arrived a day early.

"Nice, huh?" I headed for the back where the bedroom was.

"Nice isn't the word." The suite at the Velez Inn was more like an apartment rather than a hotel room. "First you take me on a jet then we're staying in this nice suite."

It was comical when my car service pulled up to the jet strip and Indigo noticed my jet fueled and ready for takeoff. I think she thought we would drive to the derby, but road trips weren't my style.

"You should know I don't do anything half-ass." She took a seat on the bench at the end of the bed. "I didn't think to get the two-bedroom suite, you good with sharing with me?" I licked my lips and eyed her.

She looked like she could pop at any moment, but hopefully, the boys would hold out for a few more weeks.

She gave me a shy grin. "It wouldn't be the first time." Her lashes batted.

"True." I looked around the room. "The races start at ten tomorrow morning, so the rest of the day is free for us." I knew which horse I was betting on and if I won, I would have a generous payout.

"Do you come here every year?"

"Sure do for the past seven or eight years."

"And do you always win?"

I grinned. "Most times, yes. The horse I bet on is my own and I make sure it's trained by the best."

Her eyes widened. "Wait, you have a horse?"

My shoulders lifted. "More so, I sponsor it and make sure it's taken care of. It gets the top care and training to prepare for this weekend every year."

"So you truly take this gambling thing serious?" She leaned back on the bed.

My lips pressed together. "Anything that has to do with my money, I take serious."

"So you don't have a gambling issue do you? I mean I know you're loaded and can afford it but I rather my kids' father not have a gambling problem."

A deep chuckle fell out my mouth. I made my way to where Indigo was sitting and stood above her. Reaching out and gripping her chin, I tilted her head upwards, bending over and claiming her lips with mine.

My tongue traced the outline of her mouth before it opened, accepting my tongue. "You have nothing to worry about," I spoke against her lips and kissed her again.

Our kiss grew deeper. When she moaned in my mouth, blood rushed down to my dick.

Pulling back, I swiped my lips with my tongue. Her stomach rumbled, causing the corner of my mouth to hike up.

"How about we get some food in you, huh?" My thumb brushed across her bottom lip.

"I'll like that."

Standing up, I headed for the desk in the room, looking through it until I found what I was looking for.

"Here's the menu, let me know what you want and I'll order room service."

I typically ate the same thing when I stayed at one of these hotels so I didn't need to look.

After giving her the menu, I walked to where my bags were so I could grab something to get more comfortable.

———

After tipping the server and closing the door behind him, I headed for the bedroom to let Indigo know the food had arrived. She decided she wanted to soak in the bath before she ate so she could relax, complaining her back was bothering her. I knew the hotel had a spa attached and made a mental note to schedule her an appointment before we left.

I stepped into the bedroom and halted when I noticed her leaning over the bed naked, looking through her suitcase. Her body had thickened so much during her pregnancy, giving her curves she didn't have before.

My dick grew in my sweats and tongue swiped across my bottom lip. I hadn't felt inside her since the day in the shower, but my shaft remembered how snug and warm she was.

Indigo was oblivious to the fact that I had stepped in the room. Slowly, I made my way to where she was standing. Indigo jumped when I pressed up against her and grabbed her wide hips.

"You scared me," she whispered, tilting her head back on my chest while I kissed on her neck. My hand ran up and down her bare skin.

"I came to tell you the food's here, but I see something I think will taste better." My teeth sank into her neck. She released a small moan.

Moving one of my hands to the front of her body, I ran it over her swollen stomach up to her large breasts and caressed them gently. Lightly, I placed kisses on her shoulder blades, tweaking her nipples between my fingers.

"Your skin is so soft." I kissed my way up her neck until I got to where it met her ear. Using the tip of my tongue, I flickered it across her flesh and pulled it into my mouth. "It taste so sweet too."

Her chest rose and body melt against me.

My hand still on her waist moved to her lower half and strummed over her clit. Her knees buckled.

Indigo widened her legs, she panted lowly, and her chest raised and fell quicker.

"I want you," she whined lowly.

Sliding my fingers across her lower lips, I groaned at how wet she was.

I released Indigo and she turned to face me. Lust filled her dilated eyes, and her cheeks flushed.

"Don't you want to eat?" I raised a brow while tugging on my bottom lip with my teeth.

"Food can wait."

I scanned over body, loving how luscious it looked. Reaching behind her, I pushed her suitcase out the way, then nodded for her to climb on the bed.

Catching my drift, Indigo quickly as her stomach allowed her climb on the bed and waited. I stripped out my sweats, down to my boxers and stepped closer to her.

"You know it's one thing I haven't done with you, that's had me curious for a while," I let her know.

Her eyes flickered to my face, and she blinked slowly. "What?"

"Scoot back," I told her.

She moved so she was in the center of the king size bed, and I climbed up behind her. Indigo watched me as I laid on my stomach, spreading her legs, and positioning myself between them.

Her orbs widened when she caught on to my intentions.

"Normally, I would wait until after we eat for desert but you look so editable right now." I kissed the inside of her thigh, and her legs jerked.

I kissed and nibbled on her meaty thighs, making my way upwards to her honey pot. I could smell her arousal and feel the heat radiating off it.

When I glanced up, she was leaning back on her elbows, her low eyes locked on me. Her mouth slightly parted.

"I should have been tasted you." I flicked my tongue over her lower lips. She moaned lowly and tossed her head back.

Spreading her lips, I moved in, inhaling her enchanting scent before diving in. Her pussy was soaked with juices, and I was thirsty. Eagerly, I devoured her pussy, using my thumb to massage her clit.

Her moans grew louder and legs threatened to close around my head. Her sex grew wetter, soaking my goatee. My tongue lapped her juices. One then two of my fingers entered her, stroking her insides.

She arched her hips into my mouth, grinding into it.

"Oh God!" she cried as her body trembled. I circled my tongue around her clit then pulled it into my mouth.

"Fuck!" Glancing up, I saw her head tossed back and eyes squeezed shut.

Indigo tasted like the sweetest peach I'd ever eaten. Her juices were endless, quenching a deep thirst inside me.

I didn't make it a habit when it came eating pussy, but with how good Indigo tasted I was ready to change that.

Eventually, Indigo was pushing my head away from her, begging me to stop while her body continued trembling.

My dick was painfully hard in my boxers. I reached down and squeezed my bulge.

Taking a few more licks of Indigo's lower lips, I pulled up and swiped my tongue over my lips.

"I should have been tasted you."

"I agree," she panted, her chest rising and falling quickly.

I kissed my way up her body, giving extra attention to her stomach.

Hovering over her, I pecked around her breasts. My tongue explored her hardened buds. She arched her back into my mouth.

Switching sides, I teased her other breast, brushing my hand across her hardened petal.

Indigo grabbed my head and pulled it upwards. She stared at me with intoxicating eyes.

"I need to feel you." Her eyes pleaded with me.

Giving her a quick nod, I sat up so I could free my hard length.

Indigo turned to her side then glanced over her shoulder. "This is more comfortable."

I didn't object. Positioning myself behind her, I held my pole and placed it at her entrance. My arm wrapped around her and I thrusted forward, invading her walls.

"Fuck!" I gritted, digging my face into her neck.

My lips pressed against it as I started stroking her slowly. She whimpered and tossed her ass back to meet my thrust.

It always felt like the first time every time I entered Indigo. She was always so tight and knowing I was the only one who'd ever experienced it always made my dick harder.

Each time I pushed deeper into her it was like a drug, lulling me to euphoria. Her moans grew louder and she gripped my wrist tightly, digging her nails into my skin.

Her walls clenched around me and my balls drew up.

My movements quickened. Passion fluttered up my spine and a hot ache grew in my throat.

Never had sex felt like this for me before. It felt as if her pussy was molded for my dick.

I sucked on her skin, feeling my orgasm grow near. A low growl escaped my throat and I bit into her flesh. A raw sense of possession took over me. My strokes became quicker. I squeezed her full breasts and Indigo's body tensed as she came with me following behind her.

———

Indigo and I cleaned up and had to end up reheating our food up. Now we were sitting in the living room with some TV show she was currently binging on Netflix playing on the TV.

Indigo hadn't said much since we cleaned up and got settled. It was clear something was on her mind, however. She would sneak peeks at me but wouldn't say anything.

I shoved the final piece of my steak into my mouth and chewed slowly, turning my head to look at her. She had laughed at whatever happened on the TV.

"I swear Mike Epps and Wanda knew what they were doing when they created this show." She scooped up the cheesecake she had brought up with her food and shoved it in her mouth.

My eyes stayed locked on her. She didn't get dress, instead she opted for the hotel's robe.

Eventually, she turned her head to look at me. "Why are you staring at me like that?" An amused expression formed on her face.

I scanned her face over. "I just wanna make sure you're good." She pushed her locs out her face and smiled. "After what we just did, I feel amazing, trust me." She flashed a grin.

"I aim to please." Her stare soften.

"There is something I actually been thinking about." She gnawed on her bottom lip. "Once we get back, I think I'm going to take my maternity leave."

"Really?" My brows raised.

I didn't have an issue with that, but Indigo had made it known she wanted to work up until she wasn't able anymore.

"Yeah." She sighed. Her lips poked out. "I wanted to work until I gave birth, but being on my feet all day is starting to take a toll on me. My doctor wants to induce me early instead of waiting the whole forty weeks so that only gives us a couple weeks until the twins arrive. I just feel like it'll be better if I start preparing now. My mom told me I'm nesting or something like that."

My shoulders lifted. "That's fine with me. If I had it my way you would have been stopped working."

She rolled her eyes. "That leads me to my next point. I don't know when I'll go back to work. Maternity leave varies from job to job or course, I think mine offers twelve weeks, but I don't know if I'll be ready to leave them that soon. I want to breast feed and bond with them as much as I can. I know you'll have to go back to work, but I don't want to have to rely on others babysitting them so young."

My hands crossed in my lap and eyes squinted. "So what are you saying to me exactly, Indigo?"

She pushed a heavy breath out. "I think I want to take six months off from working to stay at home. It'll give me enough time to adjust to motherhood and after that, I want to go back to work. I don't know if my job will be waiting for me, but I'll worry about that later. I'm not even sure I want to drive almost an hour out every day once the kids get here anyways. I do want to go back to work because I love what I do and I love working in a lab."

"I have no issue with that. You've barely touched the account I set up for you. The money will last you for a lifetime. You honestly don't have to work again, which I know you're not going for." I tossed my hands up, noticing the scold forming on her face. "The point is whatever you want to do, I'll support. I'm not going to be upset because you want to stay home with our kids."

She inhaled a sharp breath and scratched her chin. "I just hate sitting on my ass and relying on someone else. It's never been me and I'm used to working. I don't know if I know how not to."

"Once the twins get here, I'm sure you won't think that. You'll have your hands full." She snickered.

"Yeah, I guess you're right."

Her forehead creased for a second and mouth pouted as if there was something else on her mind, but it passed, and she was smiling again.

"I'm glad me and you finally seem to be on the same page, Silas. It brings me comfort when it comes to our kids." She rubbed her stomach, bringing my attention to it.

A fire lit in my chest. The pull I felt for Indigo seemed to grow stronger each day. Her independence was attractive to me. The fact that she still would rather work instead of being a stay-at-home mom, was slightly aggravating to me, but I admired it at the same time. She didn't depend on my money or want to be taken care of, and those facts alone made me want to show my appreciation to her.

Chapter Twenty-Three

Indigo

I was a coward.

Last night, I wanted to question the status of me and Silas, but instead I shifted the conversation to me going on early maternity leave. The two of us needed to have a conversation about where we stood. Although our co-parenting relationship was going well so far, I felt like we were past that. In my gut I wanted more between us, I just wasn't sure if Silas felt the same.

This was unchartered territory for me. Formulas and chemical equations made sense to me, dating didn't. Part of me hated I'd cut myself off from it for so long because I was too old to be so inexperienced.

Lifting my head, I watched Silas as he stared out the window of the room we were in. I had never been to a horse race before, but from what I could see it was a big deal. The suite we were in came equipped with wings, finger sandwiches, champagne, beer, and soft drinks. There were three other people inside the box with us, who Silas knew. Apparently, they had their own horses they were betting on. The crowd below us was wild, yelling and cheering loudly as the horses ran the track.

"Jake, I told you, you should have betted with me and not against."

Silas looked at the middle-aged man in the seats across from us, with a cocky grin.

Jake turned to face Silas, sneering at him. "It isn't over until it's over."

"You just better hope he's wrong or you're on the couch," his wife next to him commented, her eyes locked on the race.

I bit back a snicker as he turned, giving her a blank look.

"Both of you can relax. I'll come out victorious, just like last year," Katherine spoke from behind us.

Apparently, the three always had this pissing match every year when the derby came about. Silas had mentioned there were normally a few others who got private suites to watch this year. He wanted to be able to rub his winnings in these two particular face—his words not mine.

Although the three were competitive with one another, everyone greeted me nicely.

My eyes shifted back to the track. I wasn't sure what to expect, but it had turned out to be eventful. Thankfully, the weather was nice. The sun was shining brightly and there was a small breeze every so often.

I lowered my hand onto the arm rest next to me, not realizing Silas had placed his hand on top of it as well. My eyes shot open when I noticed a spark shoot up my arms.

I went to move my hand but was surprised when Silas stopped me.

Turning my head to look at him, I saw his eyes were now locked on me. My heart hammered inside me.

"Are you enjoying yourself?" he questioned lowly, stroking the top of my hand with his thumb.

Something I couldn't place planted itself in his orbs.

My tongue suddenly felt heavy in my mouth. I nodded and gripped his hand securely. "Thank you for inviting me. Who knew watching horses' race could be so exciting."

One side of his mouth lifted. "You haven't seen anything yet, just wait until the results come in and the drunk idiots get mad."

For a second, I shifted my eyes down to the general crowd. I could envision what he spoke just based on how rowdy everyone was already.

"I can only imagine." Silas went back to watching the track, but his hand stayed stroking mine softly. I wasn't sure if he was aware of what he was doing and I didn't want to bring attention to it. His hands were large and strong, soft as well.

With my free hand, I reached for my drink, needing something to clench my now parched throat. Fear crept inside me, but I tried to ignore it. I found myself growing fonder of him. A small part of me thought it might've been deeper than that, but I refused to acknowledge that part.

My heart fluttered and tightness filled my chest. A conversation needed to be had and soon, The more time I spent with Silas, the more I felt like I was creeping towards the edge of a cliff. Soon, I felt like I would slip and be unable to catch myself.

Silas squeezed my hand and I thought it was because he wanted my attention, but when I looked at him, I saw his eyes were locked on the track. His body sat straighter, mouth pinched together. He was focused and the look on his face sent a shiver down my spine and caused my center to ache. It was captivating, honestly.

Closing my eyes, I pushed a small breath out. I needed to get a hold of myself. I was going to blame my sudden found horniness on my pregnancy. It was as if I wanted to jump on Silas every time he was near me. My mind shifted to how his tongue felt on my pussy last night, causing me to squeeze my thighs tightly.

Shaking my head, I pushed those thoughts away. Now wasn't the time to think about how I was falling for this man or the things I wanted him to do to my body.

———

Silas kissed my forehead and grinned widely. "You're my good luck charm. I'm convinced," he bragged as he guided us to the front of the track.

I wasn't sure exactly how much he won but by the way he was

cheesing and the disappointment of the others, it must have been a generous amount.

We got to the front and the car service Silas had hired for us while we were here was already waiting for us.

Once inside, I got lost in my thoughts for a moment. Silas was tapping away on his phone. We would be leaving tomorrow and from there it would be a countdown until the twins got here. I planned on putting my notice in at the lab when we returned as well. I felt bad leaving so soon since I was still new and Dr. Foe gave me a chance fresh out of school. Hopefully, he wouldn't hold it against me. I would miss learning from him and working with him.

"Where would you like to eat?" Silas's voice knocked me out my thoughts.

"What?"

He was staring at me with curiosity bouncing in his eyes. "I know the food at the track wasn't enough for you. Where would you like to eat?"

I didn't answer right away. My attention went behind him and a smile lifted on my face. "I'm actually not hungry right now, but I would like to go there." I pointed to the park we were passing.

Silas looked behind him and turned back to me, frowning. "The park?"

I nodded. "Dr. Hill said physical activity will be good for me these next couple weeks. We can walk around that pond."

Silas's forehead creased and his brows pulled together.

I bit back the smile on my face, seeing he wanted to turn my choice down, but shockingly he let the driver know to head to the park.

Silas helped me out the back of the truck once it was parked and spoke to the driver for a few minutes before turning towards me.

"Shall we." He held his hand out to me.

With a small smile on my face, I placed my hand in his and we headed for the pond on the side of the park. The path around the pond had a few people walking it some with their dogs and others solo. The park was full of families.

I peeked at Silas. I knew this was something he wouldn't consider, normally, but I was going to enjoy this moment with him.

"Are you gonna tell me what's been on your mind?" Silas asked me after a few minutes.

I blinked a couple times slowly, unsure how to answer. "What do you mean?" I licked my lips.

"Since last night I noticed something on your mind, but instead of telling me what it was you kept it to yourself. At the track I saw the same look and even now. Is something the matter? Did I do something to offend you?"

The twins were resting currently, but that didn't stop butterflies from fluttering inside my stomach. Heat raised through my body, shooting to the tip of my ears.

Now was the perfect time to bring up my concerns; I just wasn't sure if I wanted to hear his answer.

There was a bench coming up and instead of passing it, I pulled on Silas' hand to guide him over to it.

I gnawed on the inside of my cheek and folded my hands in my lap once we were seated.

"I actually need to talk to you." Batting my lashes, I glanced up at him with my head slightly tilted to the side.

Silas stayed quiet, giving me the go ahead to continue.

It was now or never.

Inhaling a deep breath, I pushed my worries away and spoke again. "I want to know what exactly we're doing. I know at first you said relationships weren't for you and that you didn't want to be tied down. I'm not even trying to pressure you into anything, but you can't deny the past month or so things with us have changed. You're more attentive and I'm trying to not be so headstrong. Not to mention, sex with us seems more intimate than it was before. The twins will be here soon and I would like us to be on the same page. We agreed to co-parenting but I honestly would like to try and maybe see if we could give our sons a real chance at a family. If it doesn't work then no harm done, we can just co-parent like normal, but I'm not scared to admit I want more."

Once I started, I couldn't stop. My words came rushing out while my heart pounded like a drum inside me. My nerves were running wild.

A pregnant pause formed between us. Silas stared at me with a look I couldn't make out. I watched his Adam's apple move up and down as he swallowed then my attention went to his lips when his tongue swiped across the bottom one.

I was beginning to grow nervous thinking maybe I'd jumped the gun.

"So you noticed it too." He finally spoke after a few agonizing seconds.

Drawing my eyebrows together, I waited for him to go further. "The last thing I expected was to get so invested in what this was. I planned on helping with the twins but keeping our relationship strictly about them." He flexed his hands; his orbs grew more intense as if he was staring into my soul. "Somewhere along the line, being around you became easy and the thought of us being more didn't seem so…appalling."

My stomach flipped when he paused again while my skin prickled with goosebumps. "I'm not saying I want to rush into a relationship. I'm still trying to come to terms that my view on everything has shifted. I can't say I won't try to control things or draw back at times, but if you're willing to be patient with me, I'm willing to see what could happen between us beyond co-parenting."

It felt like my heart was about to explode out my chest and a rush shot through my body. The conversation could have gone two ways, but I couldn't stop the happiness that filled me for it going in my favor.

"When did it change for you?"

His teeth sunk into his bottom lip and he began cracking his knuckles. His attention left mine and he watched the people passing us.

"I'm not sure, but I knew when I saw you with your boss and how you smiled at him, that my feelings for you weren't just on a co-parent level."

I inhaled a sharp breath. Silas was admitting he was jealous, and for some reason, that caused a passionate fluttering to arise on the back of my neck.

When Silas turned back to me, he reached out to grab my hand and gave it a slight squeeze. The mere touch alone sent a warming shiver through me.

Silas dipped his head and pressed his lips on mine. It was slow and light like the breeze passing through us.

"You are mine." His confession lit a fire in my chest. "These two are mine." His free hand went to my stomach. My skin tingled.

"I grew up an only child which makes me selfish as hell at times." His stare grew scorching. My mouth parted and my heart continued pounding in a thundering beat. "Meaning I don't share what's mine, Indigo. I hope you can handle what you unlocked inside me."

Chapter Twenty-Four

Silas

My fingers sank into Indigo's meaty hips while I pumped in and out of her. Her arch increased and sweet moans filled the room.

Sweat beaded on my forehead and mouth pinched as I tried not to cum. Her heat was hugging my dick tightly, soaking it in her juices.

Ripples formed in her ass as it bounced back against my pelvis.

The moment we got back to our room, I was on her. Last night I knew something was going on with her, but she refused to address it right away. Part of me had a feeling what she wanted to talk about. The way Indigo started looking at me was different from the beginning. It was softer and more passionate. Her orbs would become lighter and voice honeyed when we talked. What I wasn't expecting was for my feelings towards her to shift.

The thought of having someone with me consistently never appealed to me. The thought of being in a relationship used to make me feel locked down and like I would be controlled again. Since I'd been around Indigo, I hadn't felt like that. She was easy to deal with, and I enjoyed being around her.

Indigo's body trembled and her pussy grew tighter.

My balls tightened and my dick jerked inside. "Fuck!" I groaned, following behind her. My body tightened and fingers sank more into her.

Dropping my chin to my chest, I squeezed my eyes shut as my orgasm shot through me. Both of our breathing was heavy.

After a few thundering heart beats, I pulled out of Indigo slowly. Her body sagged as she rolled on her side.

I watched in awe, loving the glow from her pregnancy mixed with sweat radiating off her skin.

Hovering over her, I pushed her locs out the way and kissed the side of her damp face.

She shuttered and fluttered her eyes open.

"I can get use to this."

Chuckling, I swiped my forehead with the back of my hand.

"Ima start the shower so we can get cleaned up." I kissed her temple again before preceding to get off the bed.

Indigo muttered something I couldn't make out, and her eyes closed again.

My heart danced in an offbeat rhythm the longer I watched her. A warm sensation shot through my body and wrapped around me as if a heated blanket was turned on. Thoughts of previous conversations I had with Lawson played in my mind. Maybe he wasn't too far off when he mentioned having an in-house family wasn't all too bad.

———

"Mrs. Newton, you can't just barge in there!" my secretary complained as my office door was shoved open.

My face slacked after lying eyes on my mom. She strutted in with not a hair out of place, her nose up, and looking like she didn't have a care in the world.

The peace I felt from my weekend of winnings and with Indigo slowly started to disappear as I took her in.

"It's fine. This won't take long," I let my secretary know.

My mom glared at me then turned to face my secretary. "You can go now."

My secretary muttered something while closing my door behind her. I pushed a deep breath out and mentally counted to ten.

"Silas," she started, approaching my desk.

"What can I do for you, Mother?" My attention went back to the forms I was working on before she barged in.

"First you could show me some respect! I shouldn't have any issues with coming to visit my son."

"She was doing her job by stopping uninvited people from bothering me," my tone clipped.

"I'm your mother, Silas."

I brought my middle finger and thumb to my eyes, rubbing them and sagged my shoulders.

"What can I do for you, Mother?" I questioned again, this time giving her my attention.

"We need to talk about your actions at the charity event last weekend." She took a seat in one of the chairs in front of my desk, crossed her legs at the knee, and placed her purse on her lap.

"I said all I needed to say that night. What else is there to discuss?"

"Besides the fact that you embarrassed me and your father by—"

"If you bring up Indigo, I will call security and personally have them escort you out!" My hand around the pen in it tightened.

My mom's lips pursed together. "Silas, honey." This time her voice was softer. I knew this trick though. My mom was manipulative, and I'd learned that early in life. When she seen force didn't work, she liked to work off your emotions.

"No," I shut down, "I'm not going to sit here and let you tell me how you don't approve of Indigo. She is having my kids, very soon at that, and there is nothing you or anyone else can do about it. Not to mention, who I choose to be involved with has nothing to do with you. I've told you countless times to leave the subject alone and you refuse, so now I'm going to end it all. For here on out, I don't want you around me, Indigo, or our kids."

My mom went to object but I held my hand up. "This isn't up for debate. I will not have anyone who isn't happy for me, in my life or around my family. Indigo might not come from a prestigious family but she's one of the best women I've ever encountered. She's respectable, smart, loving, and if I'm being honest, *too* good for *me*. I will not continue to allow you to belittle her and hurt her. I love you, but I'll have to love you from a distance."

My mom's mouth gapped and this was the one of those rare occasions I left her speechless. "So you're choosing that woman over your own mother!" Her voice heightened a pitch.

"If that's how you see it then yes." My face stayed blank. "I allowed you to dictate my life for too long and ran away from a relationship even longer in fear that I would lose control on how I want to live. I'm not living my life like that anymore. You can live how you want, but without me in it."

You would have thought I struck my mother by how her head cocked back. A pregnant pause passed between us. "Well then." She stood up. For a second, it looked like a remorseful look passed through her face, but it quickly disappeared. "When that women uses you up and spits you out don't come running to me crying." She tilted her chin.

A beep from the intercom gained my attention before I could respond. "Mr. Newton, you have a Tiara Jenkins on line one."

Indigo's mom calling caught me off guard.

My mom's eyes narrowed. "Put her through," I replied. "Have a great day, Mother." I picked up the phone.

My mom scoffed and spun on her heels, storming towards the door. Her heel clicked roughly on the floor.

Shaking my head, I leaned back in my seat.

"Hello, Tiara. What can I do for you?"

————

"You've finally come to the light, huh?" Lawson smirked, sitting back in his high-top chair and staring at me.

My hand tightened on my glass and cut to where Rhys was throwing his darts.

"I'm giving it a try." My eyes went back to him.

"You'll see, Si, life is more enjoyable having a permanent partner to share it with."

My mouth turned upside down. "I wouldn't go that far."

"You might as well. You two are together now, right?" Caspian spoke up.

I rubbed the back of my neck. I couldn't answer that question because I didn't know if me and Indigo were together. She confessed she had feelings for me and I told her mine, but I wasn't sure if that meant we were in a relationship.

"I'm not sure." My nose scrunched.

"You too old to be so confused about your relationship," Rhys approached the table and spoke.

I turned and mugged him. "All this shit is new for me. I went from sleeping with who the hell I wanted, to having twins and having one girl. Shits not gonna be clear right away."

"I'm just fucking with you man, relax. I'm glad you're finally getting over your issues and settling down." Rhys gripped my shoulder.

"Sounds like you might want that too," Lawson commented.

Rhys shrugged and took a seat. "Been thinking about it. I'm the oldest out all of us, and I think it's time I start trying to settle down and start a family of my own."

"When the fuck did all y'all become so boring? We're millionaires, we have the world at our disposal. Why settle so soon?" Caspian complained.

Lawson shook his head. "So soon? We're in our thirties man. Time isn't going backwards."

Lawson's phone vibrated on the table in front of him. He picked it up and peeked at the screen. His face balled up and he shot up. "Speaking of, I need to head home."

"We're not finished," Caspian grumbled.

"Sorry, fellas, wifey calls." He collected his things, waved, and headed for the door.

I chuckled and shook my head. "Is that what you want? Being at a woman's beck and call?" Caspian spun and faced me.

"You sound like a hater, man." Rhys gave him a blank stare.

"I'm just saying. Maybe the family life isn't what everyone wants."

"Out of everyone, I would think you would be the main one wanting one." Caspian grew quiet. His face pinched and he downed his drink.

"Because of what I went through, is the main reason I'm in no rush." He snatched up his darts and turned for the board.

Rhys and I shared a look but didn't comment back. Caspian had lost his parents in an accident when we were in college. He didn't speak on it and hardly showed it affected him, but we all knew it did.

Instead of dwelling on the same subject, Rhys switched it, speaking on the upcoming football season. Caspian seemed thankful for the change. Once he got back to the table, his mood heightened back.

While he and Rhys spoke on who they felt would go all the way this year, I went to my phone and saw I had a message. Opening it, I noticed it was a picture message from Indigo, showing her stomach.

We only had two weeks until she got induced and then the twins would be here. Time was winding down and both of us were nervous, her more so than me. While at the derby, I made sure to have Fiona finish getting the twins' rooms together. It was still hard to believe in fourteen days, I would be a father.

Chapter Twenty-Five

Indigo

"We're going to miss you around here, Indigo," Dr. Foe commented as we finished up for the day.

It was my official last day of working at the lab and it was bittersweet. I had learned so much these short couple of months. It never felt like I was working when I was here either, still I was ready to prepare for my kids.

My back had been bothering me more, I was more tired, my ankles were swelling. It was time to take it easy.

"I want to thank you for taking a chance with me, Greg. I'm sorry I couldn't be here longer." I felt bad. I knew my mentor went out her way to help me secure the job here and me getting pregnant wasn't in the plans.

He waved me off. "Nonsense. You're about to start a new journey. A beautiful one. If I had a chance at that again, I would take it in a heartbeat." My heart hurt for him.

The day he told me about his wife, I stopped lusting after my boss. Although, I still found him attractive it felt wrong wanting him and knowing what he went through with his wife.

I rubbed my stomach. "I know you said you want to take an extended leave once your sons arrive, but we've enjoyed having you here. When you're ready, come talk to me, and we'll have a place for you." My brows shot up.

"Really?" He grinned and nodded.

"I don't know if you noticed but we're pretty exclusive here. I don't allow just anyone to work on my team. You're the first new addition in two years. So if you want to come back the position is yours."

Excitement shot through my body. "Thank you, Greg! I was worried what I would do when it came time to go back to work, and that helps ease my mind a lot!"

"We're family here, and family takes care of family. Enjoy mother-hood and get settled."

His words warmed my heart. I was grateful for the opportunity to come back and work under him if I chose to. I knew it would be some time before I was ready to come back to work, but knowing my job would still be here, settled a lot of nerves inside me.

"Silas, are you going to tell me why I couldn't stay in my bed like I originally planned?" I whined as he led me to the brick building in front of us.

"That would ruin the surprise, wouldn't it?" My pout deepened.

"I don't want a surprise, I want my bed!" I didn't feel like being out and about. It was like once the twins knew it was growing closer to their eviction date they started showing out more and dragging my body down with them.

"I promise it'll be worth me dragging you out the house." He dipped down and pecked my forehead.

The frown didn't leave my face.

Not only was my body sore and aching, but my attitude had been shit the past couple days too. I wasn't trying to be snappy with anyone, but I was ready for these kids to be out of me. I enjoyed my pregnancy up until this point, but I was tired of being miserable.

Silas opened the door and allowed me in first before following behind me. His hand went to the small of my back and he led me down a narrow hallway.

"What the hell is this place?" I looked around.

He stayed quiet and stopped in front of one of the closed doors on the wall.

"Silas," I warned.

A crooked grin formed on his face and he pulled the door open. I gave him a hesitant look and he nodded for me to proceed.

The moment I stepped through the door into the alternate room, my mouth dropped.

"Surprise!" My eyes bucked.

The hall I stepped in was decorated in a safari theme. In the back were two large gold thrones with a gold, white, and light green balloon arch over it. On one side, I could see a dessert table and a buffet of food. The other, had a bunch of tables and chairs. Near the thrones, a pile of gifts were stacked up on one side and the other had a light green background, another balloon arch, and the names Welcome Ezekiel and Isaac in a banner above. After we got back from the derby, I brought up the fact that we didn't have names for the twins and we spent more than an hour debating on what to call them before coming to a conclusion.

"Mommy," I whispered when she approached me.

I saw the room filled with my family and friends.

"I know you said you didn't want one, but you deserved it." She grabbed my face and held it tightly.

Tears clouded my eyes. "You shouldn't have done this."

She released me and my dad walked up to us. "I didn't. Well not really. Silas got a planner to put it all together, I just made sure everyone showed up." Sitting up, I stared at Silas who had a bashful look on his face.

I stepped closer to him and wrapped my arms around his waist, hugging him tightly.

"Thank you," I mumbled against his chest.

His strong arms wrapped around me and he kissed the top of my head.

"About time you got here," my sister's voice sounded, causing me to pull back. Audrey had approached us with her.

"Aren't you glad I made you dress up?" Silas taunted.

I snickered. I tried wearing a pair of his sweats and a t-shirt, but he refused to let me leave the house like that. Instead, he insisted I wore this white and gold dress and even had some gold accessories with it. He proclaimed he was out and saw the dress and thought of me and the worker threw in the jewelry. Now I saw that wasn't true.

"Come, come. Say hello to your guests and then we can get started," my mom suddenly said, grabbing my arm.

"Slow down," I complained, waddling behind her.

I waved to Fiona who was sitting at one of the tables. I was surprised to even see Zarinah, Kimmie, Inayah, and Aspen in the audience. We kept in touch after the cookout so I was glad they came.

Although I wanted to spend the day in my bed, I couldn't lie and say I wasn't happy my family and friends went out their way and threw me a shower. Seeing how loved my boys were had me in tears multiple times during the evening.

"Are you having a good time?" Silas asked while I stuffed my face. I was happy to see my mom and a few of my aunts had cooked instead of catering.

I nodded, not letting up on the chicken I was eating.

He chuckled. "Next time you gone accept my surprise without all the questions." I cut my eyes at him and licked some juices off my lips.

"I wouldn't go that far."

The sound of a shutter gained my attention. I turned and saw Grayson, the photographer my mom had hired, had taken a picture. "Nooooo, not of me eating," I groaned.

"Ima need that blown up," Silas let him know.

Grayson grinned. "Will do."

Rolling my eyes, I went back to my plate. I didn't expect my family to go all out like they did. When I found out they hired an actual photographer to do videography and photos for the event, I was blown away. I shouldn't have been shocked though; if my mom had Silas' help then nothing was going to be half-done.

"Rich baby daddy. Your party planner did her thing tonight." My sister came up to our table and took a seat. I didn't even bother correcting her. Silas didn't seem to mind the nickname either.

"I'm glad to hear it."

"Yeah, even I can say I'm impressed," my brother commented.

He would be leaving soon and I was sad. I hated he chose to go far away for school, but I was proud of him at the same time.

The evening went on and after eating, everyone wanted to take pictures with me and Silas as well as get some of us alone. Of course, my mom went overboard with the family shots, making sure we all got many angles and poses. I didn't complain though, since I didn't take maternity pictures I would cherish these ones.

Right before the night ended, we did the presents and it was over-whelming seeing how many there were.

"Where is all this going to go?" I complained as they loaded the truck. I was sure a couple cars were going to be needed.

I was beyond grateful for all the love we were shown, but they went overboard with the buying.

"Between both our places we'll make room."

"This is why you need a house," my sister commented.

"Charley," I warned.

"Mhm, I think she's right." Silas stroked his chin.

"No, she's not." I turned to face him. "The condo is enough for now. We'll make it work."

Silas stared at me blankly and just as I was about to speak again, he smirked.

"Okay."

The way he said it let me know I would have to assure him I didn't need a house right now.

After saying our goodbyes and thanking everyone for coming, Silas helped me in the car and started for our house with my parents behind us.

"Thank you for today." I glanced over at him. Tonight had me even more excited to meet my sons.

He glanced at me. "No need to thank me. When your mom came to me about it, I didn't second guess it. You deserve to be celebrated."

A smirk ticked on my face. "I love the space we're in." I closed my eyes on laid my head on the headrest. "I hope we only get closer," I yawned and confessed sleepily.

During the past five months our relationship had grown so much. It always caused my heart to swell thinking about where we started and where we were now. Since coming back from the derby, Silas seemed to be more open with the two of us progressing and we even spent every night sleeping together between our two houses. The experience was new for the both of us, but it was soothing to me.

I started dozing off, feeling the effects of today catching up with me. "Me too, baby. We will," Silas let me know as sleep consumed me.

Epilogue

Epilogue

I ndigo didn't know how people had multiple kids. After she was admitted into the hospital and was induced, she knew she was two and done. The contractions had damn near took her out and the actual birth had her cursing out everyone in the room.

While her mom seemed unaffected by her outburst, Silas looked like he was going to pass out the moment the first twin made his appearance.

She was in labor for twelve hours before she was finally ready to push and those were the most miserable hours of her life. She couldn't eat, her nerves were bad, and the pain was unbearable.

"Which one is this, again?" Charley asked, staring at her nephew in awe.

Indigo lifted slightly to check. "Isaac."

Her body was worn out, and she was grateful her family had been here, but she was ready to kick them out and sleep. The nurses had let her know they would be in soon so she could try feeding the twins. She wanted to breastfeed and hoped they latched.

"How do you know?"

"The bracelet."

Indigo knew people were going to confuse the twins so she had

208

gotten them colored bracelets to place on their wrist to help tell who's who.

"So this cutie is Ezekiel," her mom gushed.

Indigo knew once she was out the hospital, she would have trouble keeping her mom away. She could already tell by how bright her eyes were she was in love with her grandkids.

"Can't believe you made me a grandpa. I still got a few golden years left," her dad commented.

"Daddy please." Charley bunched her nose up, causing a tired giggle to leave Indigo.

Silas had come up to the bed and took a seat on the edge. His hand went to her locs and he pushed them out her face.

"You did great," he let her know.

He might have looked like he would pass out, but he was there every step of the way supporting her. She was sure she had almost crushed his hand by how hard she was squeezing it.

"Thank you. Hopefully, I wasn't too bad." A lazy grin formed on his face.

He smirked and shook his head. "You weren't completely unbearable." He stroked her hand lightly and stared at her with a soft expression on his face.

"Okay let me hold him," Audrey complained to Charley.

Twenty minutes went by before the nurse came in to start the feedings and the family decided to leave. Unfortunately, Indigo's brother had left and wasn't able to stay for the arrival of his nephews, but he promised to be back as soon as he could to meet them.

"I think they're gonna look like me," Silas commented, holding one of his sons in his face.

Indigo frowned and glanced down at the twin feeding from her at the moment. Thankfully, both latched.

"It's too early to tell."

Silas gave her a knowing look. "Trust me, they're going to take after me."

Indigo rolled her eyes and grinned. "At least you're attractive."

Silas laughed and gave his son another look. Both parents seemed to get lost in their sons, but unable to believe they were finally here.

"Would you do it again?" Silas suddenly asked her.

Indigo lifted her eyes and stared at him. She glanced at the son he was holding and gave a toothless grin. Her heart tripled in size.

"In a heartbeat."

———

One month later…

"They're fed and sleep." Indigo yawned as she stepped into Silas' bedroom and climbed onto his bed. He insisted they stayed with him at night so that he could help her easier and this was the first time she didn't fight him.

The twins were officially a month old and although she loved being a mother, having two kids to take care of was a lot. She was glad that Silas took his role as a father seriously and stepped up the moment they brought they twins home. She wasn't sure how he would be once they got here but so far things were good.

She also had her family who was a big help, especially her mom. Tiara didn't hesitate to be a listening ear or helping hand.

Silas was on his laptop with his back against his headboard, studying something intensely.

"What are you looking at?"

Indigo went to glance over and Silas rushed to close his laptop. "Just some work stuff." He looked up at her. She gave him a curious look.

"Whatever." She shrugged and grabbed her phone, unlocking it and going to her social media apps.

Silas watched her silently. Indigo seemed to be a natural mother. She jumped right into the role without any issues or complaints. He knew being the main source of the twins' food was a lot for her. Isaac took a bottle sometimes which made it easy for Silas to help, but Ezekiel refused it completely. When he first handled the twins, he was a nervous reck. He had no idea how to change diapers or hold them, but she made sure to help him.

He hadn't spoken to his parents since they were born. Neither of them even bothered to reach out. It stung at first but Silas had come to terms his parents were stuck in their ways and there was nothing he could do about it.

"Oh wow," Indigo voiced.

"What's wrong?"

"Look." She flipped the phone in his direction.

Silas furrowed his brows and studied it. "Shit."

There was an article about how Ria and Deacon were caught up in a love triangle. Apparently, one of his mistresses was claiming to be having his child.

"That could have been you caught up in all that," Indigo joked with a snicker in her voice.

Silas frowned. "I was too smart to get caught up like that."

She tossed the phone to the side and turned so she was facing him. "The twins are proof that's not true." Her lashes batted and lips pouted out.

Silas licked his lips and scanned her over. She still held some weight from the twins, but her new body looked good on her. Her breast were full in the tank top she was wearing and Silas was itching to put them in his mouth.

"Still don't know how that happen." He tugged on his bottom lip.

"Aren't you glad it did, though?"

His head tilted and he reached out and stroked her arm. His head lowered and he pecked her lips. "I am."

Indigo's smile grew. "I'm also happy you decided to give me and you a chance." Her eyes beamed.

Silas moved his laptop, placing it on his nightstand, then turned back to Indigo. His hand went to the back of her neck and he pulled her face close to his. His lips found hers and he kissed her deeply.

His tongue found its way inside her mouth and he traced the recess of her mouth.

Indigo closed her eyes and moaned, turning her head slightly.

Silas still couldn't believe this was his life now. So much had changed for him in just a short amount of months. He no longer fought his feelings for Indigo or what the two had created. It brought him great joy knowing he finally had someone in his life to show him what a *real* family looked like.

The end!

More Tay Mo'Nae

Standalones:

4 Ever Down With Him
He Ain't Your Ordinary Bae
Overdosed off a Hood Boys Love
These H*es Ain't Loyal
These H*es Doin' Too Much
These H*es Actin' Up
When Love Becomes A Need
When Love Becomes A Reason
When Love Becomes A Purpose
This Heart Plays No Games
This Heart Still Holds You Down
Riskin' It All For A Bad Boy
Rescued By His Love
Tempted Off His Love
DND: Caught Up In His Love
Imperfect Love
Got It Bad For An Atlanta Boss

Novellas:

Series:

His Love Got Me On Lock
My Love Is Still On Lock
Addicted To My Hitta
Serenity and Jax: A Houston Hood Tale
A Houston Love Ain't Never Been So Good: Yung & Parker
A Bad Boy Captured My Heart
Down To Ride For An ATL Goon
Still Down To Ride For An ATL Goon
In Love With A Heartless Menace
Turned A Good Girl Savage
Finessed His Love
She Got A Thing For A Dope Boy
& Then There Was You 1-2

Maple Hills:

The Sweet Spot
Strokin' The Flame Within' Her Heart
A Blind Encounter

Butter Ridge Falls:

Remember The Time
Can't Help But Love You
Chocolate Kisses
Tattoo Your Name On My Heart
Capture My Love
Aisha & Gage: Wedding Special
It's Always Been You

New Haven:

Drunk in Love
Fell For The Wrong One

Pikemoore Falls:

Three's A Crowd

The Parker Sisters:

Made in the USA
Middletown, DE
02 May 2023

29914851R00124